Madigan's Mistake

Madigan had really done it this time. Over almost twenty years as a U.S. Marshal he had made plenty of mistakes and faced the music, but this time he'd gone too far. He'd shot the favourite son of a Washington senator.

There were always villainous enemies out to get Madigan but even he was out of his depth fighting the wrath of the aroused senator. First there was jail and then his break-out, which led to the greatest danger of all. Now Madigan was a fugitive, fair game for law and enemies alike.

Dodging the bullets left him little time to try and redeem himself. And if he couldn't he was finished . . . in more ways than one.

Madigan's Mistake

HANK J. KIRBY

A Black Horse Western

ROBERT HALE · LONDON

© Hank J. Kirby 2006
First published in Great Britain 2006

ISBN-10: 0-7090-7934-6
ISBN-13: 978-0-7090-7934-7

Robert Hale Limited
Clerkenwell House
Clerkenwell Green
London EC1R 0HT

Typeset by Derek Doyle & Associates, Shaw Heath.
Printed and bound in Great Britain by
Antony Rowe Limited, Wiltshire

CHAPTER 1

ALWAYS AN OPTION

Kimble shoved the man ahead of him down the short passage leading to the rear of the saloon. He opened the door and dragged the heavily breathing cowboy into the darkness of the yard.

Weird shadows were flung about by the stacked crates, and empty beer kegs and bottles rattled underfoot with a scattering of other rubbish. Kimble pushed the staggering man roughly against the wall, held him there by his right hand.

'You're . . . hurtin',' the cowboy grunted, futilely trying to prise free Kimble's hand.

Kimble was young, big and strong. The man didn't have a chance. 'Not the most salubrious place for an interrogation, Freer, but it'll do – I want to know where you took McLaren.' He suddenly shook the man roughly. 'I know you guided him across the sierras.'

Freer swore softly, the words slurred – *but were they slurred less than before?* Kimble thought with sudden alarm. *Could this snake only be pretending to be drunk. . . ?*

'Dunno wha' y'r talkin' about. Dunno no Mc-whosit!'

Kimble hesitated, then drove a fist into Freer's midriff, turning his head as a gust of beer-laden breath hit him in the face. As he did so, he caught the fading wedge of light as the rear door of the saloon closed – and a fleeting glimpse of a darker mass against the piled crates.

Kimble's heart thudded: someone had come out and was hiding in the shadows. . . . He dropped to one knee, palming up his sixgun as flame stabbed from the direction of the crates. Freer gagged and fell across him, knocking him sprawling even as he fired. His shot went wild and the gun over there crashed twice more. Then the door was kicked open and he briefly glimpsed a large, crouching shape before he was half-blinded by the muzzle flash of the gun in the newcomer's hand. There was a yell, splintering wood, and tumbling crates. A man lurched into sight, falling face down, as the rescuer came all the way out of the saloon, kicking the door closed behind him.

He ran forward as Kimble desperately started to get to his feet, grabbing the Colt that had slipped from his hand. The man cannoned into him, knocked him aside roughly and went past him to where Freer lay in a half-sitting position against the base of the wall.

'Freer! Freer! C'mon, you're still breathing! Use what time you've got left to tell me where you took McLaren!' There was a sodden thud and a choking moan and Freer gagged.

Kimble lurched to his feet, came forward and grabbed the crouching man by the shoulder. 'The man's dying, Bronco! Leave him be!'

'Get away from me, Kimble!' US Marshal Bronco Madigan growled, without looking around. 'If you'd done your job properly, we'd know where McLaren was holed-up by now.'

'*We?* I thought this was my assignment!'

Madigan turned his head and light from the now open doorway, crowded with gawkers, showed the hard planes of his face, the trail-grimed stubble and the sun-reddened eyes. Kimble felt a lurch in his belly: Chief Marshal Parminter wouldn't send a man like Madigan after him unless there was some solid reason.

'You're taking too long, kid,' Madigan said. Deputy US Marshal Beaumont T. Kimble stiffened. 'McLaren'll be on a boat to South America before you get a whiff of where he is.'

'I was about to find out!'

'You were about to die! Freer had you spotted the moment you walked into that bar. He wasn't as drunk as he made out. All he wanted to do was get you out here in the alley so his pard could nail you. But his pard was a lousy shot, nailed Freer instead.'

Kimble was silent. Madigan turned back to Freer, shook him again, roughly, slapping him backhanded across the grey face several times. Blood streaked across Freer's sunken cheeks.

'You're going fast, Freer, and it won't be pleasant unless you tell me where you took McLaren. Where is he?'

One more slap and Freer gasped, 'Nowhere. . .'

Then his head sagged on his chest and Madigan grunted and stood, wiping his hand on his trousers. He still held his smoking Colt.

'So, all that .. interrogation .. for nothing!' There was a note of triumph in Kimble's voice. 'You filled his last moments with pain, *all for nothing*!'

Madigan pushed past the younger marshal, flashing his badge now at the men crowding into the alley. 'US Marshal – official business. Someone get the undertaker. There're two dead men here to get rid of.'

The big marshal turned down the alley, going towards the street visible at the far end. Kimble caught up with him when they were almost entering Main and grabbed Madigan's arm. The marshal spun, slapping Kimble's hand free. 'Judas priest, kid, haven't you learned anything in the six months you've been in the field!'

Kimble felt himself flush, glad there wasn't enough light for his face to be seen, dropped his hand from the other's arm. He knew it had been a mistake to grab Madigan that way, but he wasn't about to apologize.

'Now what do we do? You've just effectively killed our last chance of finding out where McLaren is!'

'Grow up, Kimble.' Madigan's voice was weary. He turned and went out into Main.

Kimble hurried after him, came up alongside. 'Well? I asked you a question! What do we do now?'

Madigan started to cross the street towards a two storeyed frame building with a faded sign across the sidewalk awning that read *Hotel*. 'Dunno what you're aiming to do, but I'm gonna find a soft bed and have me a damn good sleep.'

Kimble stopped in his tracks as Madigan kept walking. 'But . . . you said yourself time's running out! And we still don't know where McLaren is!'

'Sure we do – Freer told us.'

'You must have better hearing than me! All I heard him say was "Nowhere" . . .'

Madigan paused with one foot on the boardwalk. Light from the oil lantern by the hotel doorway showed his crooked smile. 'That's right – Nowhere Canyon. In the north part of the sierras.'

'What!'

'Should've thought of it myself – looks like a blind canyon but there's an old Indian way out. A few white men know about it. Freer did; I do. And looks like McLaren does, too. We'll have him in custody by tomorrow sundown.'

Kimble watched Madigan enter the hotel and just as the door started to swing closed, said with a touch of unaccustomed viciousness, 'If you don't kill him first!'

'Always an option, kid, always an option.'

The Rincon stage was running late, and now it was going to be even further behind schedule.

The driver, 'Dad' Pettigrew, a legend on the Wells

Fargo runs in this part of the country, saw the fallen tree lying across the trail. The shotgun guard, a flashy kid feeling his oats, named Lefty, was dozing. Pettigrew nudged him roughly with his bony elbow.

Lefty grunted, then came awake, instantly angry. 'Goddamnit, you old galoot, I told you before – *don't jab me in the ribs with your goddamn elbow*!'

'Then stay awake,' Dad Pettigrew said, and, pointing with his long whip, added, 'We don't move that there log we're all gonna be stranded out here in the desert!'

The words brought Lefty's head swivelling to the front and he half-stood in the seat, his shotgun swinging in one hand as he leaned on the roof behind.

'Judas priest! Haul rein, you old galoot! Haul—'

There was a single rifle shot and a third eye appeared in the centre of Lefty's forehead, snapping back his head, throwing his lean, rawboned body across the roof. He poised there for a moment and then spilled off to the side, hitting the alkali with a small grey-white explosion. The coach lurched and bumped as the wheels ran over him and his body was very much out of shape when it appeared behind the skidding coach.

Passengers inside yelled and a woman screamed as they were tumbled wildly, smoke rising from the brake blocks burning against the iron rims of the locked wheels. Only Dad's expertise prevented the stage from overturning as he stood to his full height of five feet six inches, wrapping the reins around his old body, using his creaking spine as support. The team was almost on top of the tree blocking the trail

10

and the leaders started to swerve and fight in the harness, but Dad brought the vehicle to a shuddering halt with the front horses pawing air almost above the tree.

He was close enough then to see the recent marks of splintering on the base. He knew this hold-up had been planned: someone had kept pushing on that dead tree until it broke and fell across the trail. Why, he didn't know – there was no express box on board. Lefty had only been along for the peace of mind of the passengers as they were travelling through Indian country. But there was nothing of value on the stage worth stealing – sure not worth *killing* for.

Yet some son of a bitch had killed Lefty in cold blood, with some damn good shooting. . . .

'OK, folks,' Dad said with a dry throat, shouting against the cries of the angry passengers. 'We're OK now – Tree blockin' the trail. . . .'

Then he saw the man with the rifle standing atop a rock just to the left of the tree. He was a hard-looking *hombre*, dusted with alkali, boots thick with it. Pettigrew figured the man had been afoot out here for some time – likely his horse had died under him and he had seen the dustcloud of the stage and decided to get himself a ride.

'Nice drivin', mister,' the man said harshly. 'Guess you must be the famous Dad Pettigrew.'

The stage driver was still standing, holding the reins, squinting at the man whose hat hung down his back by a thong. He had sandy hair, thinning on top, and there was a reddish shadow around his jowls.

'By that accent and hair, I'd say you must be Sandy

McLaren,' retorted Pettigrew. 'A murderin' son of a bitch wanted in seven states.'

The rifleman's teeth flashed. 'Eight now.' He gestured casually to the broken, bloody body of Lefty, watched alertly as the dishevelled passengers climbed out. There were two women, an old one and a younger one who might be her daughter. There were four men, three middle-aged, one a gangling kid, well-dressed in pearly-grey suit and Derby hat to match. He looked well-fed, cocky, with a bloom on his skin, blue-eyes staring candidly at McLaren.

'Why did you shoot that feller?' the young man asked, full of confidence, and McLaren felt the hostility start to bring the bile to his throat.

He did not like rich kids – unless he could get his hands on some of their money. Then he preferred it to be a rich female kid . . . they had something to offer other than money, even if they were reluctant to part with it.

'Mebbe I'll kill you next, kid,' McLaren said, deliberately coldly and the women grabbed at each other, consternation on the faces of the middle-aged men.

The kid frowned. He was leery but not as afraid as McLaren would have liked him to be. 'Come here, kid – *come here*!'

The kid started, licked his lips and swallowed and looked as if he would defy McLaren. The driver said quickly, 'Better take it easy, McLaren. His old man's a Washington senator. . . .' He could have bitten out his tongue as soon as he said it when he saw the way the killer's face lit up.

'Well, well, well! Now, ain't that somethin' . . . Kid,

I told you to come here. You can walk across right now, or I can shoot the driver – or mebbe one of the gals – or anyone else, until you decide to do what I tell you.'

The women howled, one man blustered, 'See here!'

That was as far as he got. McLaren shot him where he stood and the older woman fainted, the young one dropping to her knees beside her, fluttering a small, scented kerchief across the old, sweating face. The other men lifted their hands higher and one snapped, 'Do what he says, feller, before he kills us all!'

'Er – yesssir,' the kid said politely, not quite so arrogant now. He lifted his hands shoulder-high and started towards McLaren, wary, cockiness fading fast.

He stopped in front of the outlaw. 'What's your name, kid?'

'Randolph Cattrell.'

McLaren suddenly laughed harshly. 'Well, I'll be! Senator Titus Cattrell your old man?'

'Yes.' The boy sounded sullen, pouting.

McLaren slapped him across the face staggering him. 'Don't take that tone with me, you little bastard! Your old man's the son of a bitch who first set the law on to me five years ago. Been tryin' to get back at him – and now here you are, walkin' right into my arms!'

Cattrell was pale now and stood looking very worriedly at the outlaw.

Then another voice – from amongst the rocks where the lone tree had once grown, said, 'Leave him be, Sandy.'

McLaren reacted swiftly. Before he even looked at the man who had spoken, he stepped forward, grabbed young Cattrell and pulled the startled kid across his body as a shield. *Then* he glanced up and saw he was covered by two rifles, the big man who had spoken in clear view, the other only partly showing between some rocks. Sun glinted from a badge on the big man's chest.

'My lucky day! Bronco Madigan! The only man I hate worse'n the goddamn senator. . . . Kid! You stop squirmin' or I'm gonna start shootin' them passengers. . . .'

Randolph Cattrell stopped struggling. When he had heard Madigan's voice, seen the badge, he had thought rescue was at hand. Now he realized McLaren was actually about to take control of the situation, with him as the pivotal point.

'Let him go, Sandy,' Madigan said, but Kimble, crouched in the rocks a few feet away could tell the big man had no real hope of the outlaw obeying. Kimble's hands were sweating against the hot stock and his lips were cracked. They had been without water for more than a day, trailing McLaren out of the sierras and into this hellish desert. He was hungry, too, weary, partly glare-blind, didn't feel confident about this deal ending satisfactorily.

Suddenly, McLaren's rifle, poking underneath Cattrell's left arm, exploded, the kid jumping. But before the echoes had died away, McLaren had levered in another shell – and Dad Pettigrew's thin, gnarled body was sprawled in the dust almost under a front wheel of the stage.

McLaren, crouching behind Cattrell's body, laughed up at Madigan. 'Tell you what I'll do, Bronco,' he said. 'I won't shoot anyone else if you put down your rifle – and tell your sidekick to do the same – deal?'

'I've never been one to feel suicidal, Sandy.'

McLaren scoffed. 'Longer you take, the more bodies'll pile up. Maybe I'll shoot one of the women this time – yeah! The old one, I guess. Might have some use for the young'n later on – Or . . .' Then the rifle barrel swung up suddenly and jammed beneath Randy Cattrell's jaw, lifting the now thoroughly frightened young man to his tiptoes.

'For God's sake, Bronco!' called Kimble standing now, rifle down at his side. 'We can't play God here!'

'Well, you do what you have to, kid,' Madigan said, his rifle still at his shoulder.

'You can't toy with other people lives like this!'

'Good advice, Bronco!' McLaren said, sounding pleased with himself. 'You got about five seconds and then someone's gonna die. . . !'

'Yeah,' Madigan said quietly. 'You.'

Then the young girl screamed and Kimble started so violently that he fell off the rock, rifle clattering. . . .

Madigan's rifle whiplashed and Randy Cattrell's pearl-grey Derby spun away and the kid slumped, pulling McLaren off-balance, blood sliding down the well-fed face as he tumbled to the dust and lay still.

Before he hit the ground, Madigan's rifle was hammering and Sandy McLaren jerked in a dance of death as the bullets ripped into his unwashed body, slamming the man around like a rag doll before he sprawled across the unmoving legs of the senator's son, whose head was lying in a spreading pool of blood.

'Christ almighty, Bronco! You've killed the boy!'

Kimble was horrified – and a man who rarely, if ever, used profanity.

Madigan frowned even as he thumbed home fresh loads into the smoking rifle.' Ah, shoot! Only meant to crease him.'

'Well, you've just made the biggest mistake of your life – you've killed the kid!'

CHAPTER 2

A BAD MISTAKE

'But, God almighty, Bren! A *senator's* son! And Titus Cattrell at that!'

Chief Marshal Miles Parminter paced back and forth across his office, something he rarely did, only in moments of extreme agitation. The steel-grey, close-cropped hair glistened like metal in the drab Washington sunlight streaming through his office windows. His big hands were clasped behind his back so tightly that they were white due to blood constriction. Beefy, thick shoulders strained at the seams of his black frock coat.

He whirled about now, only a few feet from the chair where a weary, trail-filthy Madigan sprawled, trying to keep his eyes open. He had been summoned to Washington post-haste and had travelled by horse, mule and on foot in order to pick up the train that would eventually get him to the capital after seemingly endless changes.

Parminter had a man with a buggy waiting at the

depot and Madigan knew then – if he hadn't known before – that he was in heaps of trouble. He half hitched around in the chair now to look up at the chief marshal, running a hand through his sweat-lank hair.

'Chief, I had no choice. That madman McLaren had already killed three people and he'd have finished off the rest, too, if I hadn't done something drastic.'

'I read your preliminary report and I agree – McLaren had to be stopped. We did want him alive for questioning about his tie-up with the gun runners and white slavers, but killing him seems as if it was the best thing to – in the circumstances.' Parminter's voice rose a little. 'But did you have to kill a *senator's* son to do it?'

He thrust his big head, pushed by his beefy shoulders, down towards Madigan who didn't flinch an inch. He held the angry stare easily enough.

'As I understand it, he isn't dead,' he said, in that quiet, maddening way of his, determined not to show agitation while the other almost had steam jetting from his ears and nostrils he was so mad.

Parminter stood up straight and waved a big hand. 'Only a matter of time! The doctor says he's in a coma and may never come out of it – either way, Bren, that boy is as good as dead! Only nineteen, being groomed by his father for great things and now. . . .'

He lost the words, flung up his arms and strode to the sideboy. He slopped bourbon into two glasses, spilled half of Madigan's down the marshal's shirt front as he thrust it at him. They both tossed down the high-class liquor in a single gulp. Parminter walked back to his chair behind his desk more slowly now. He leaned back, threaded his fingers in a characteristic pose, elbows resting on his thickening waist-line. 'You've no idea what hell this has stirred-up.'

'Cattrell give you a hard time, huh?'

Parminter's eye blazed. 'Well, what d'you expect! His only son, *whom he worships*, shot down in cold blood – by my top marshal! Why wouldn't he give me a bad time?'

Madigan nodded, trying to hide the yawn that wanted to stretch his jaws. 'I couldn't get at McLaren through the kid, so I figured to wing him so he'd drop and give me a crack at Sandy. That stupid damn Derby he was wearing got in the way and threw my aim out a little.'

Parminter was silent a moment or two then sighed. 'And that's what I'm supposed to tell Titus Cattrell? That it was all the fault of the new Derby hat his son was wearing? And which the Ssnator no doubt paid for!'

'Chief, I dunno what you've already told him or what you're gonna tell him, but it was a genuine mistake—'

'A bad mistake! One you'll rue for the rest of your life, Bren!'

Madigan stopped speaking at the interruption. 'You want me to go see the senator and explain?' he asked, eventually.

'*Explain*! Good God, man! What's there to explain? He already knows the circumstances. He doesn't accept them and nothing you or I can do will make him. All he sees is his son lying in a coma in hospital and he doesn't know if he's going to wake up! Or, if he does, just what he's going to be like.'

Madigan frowned. 'What's that mean?'

19

'The boy could be a half-wit, his brain permanently damaged.'

Madigan straightened, his face long and sober now. His voice was hoarse when he asked, 'That the only option?'

Parminter spread his arms. 'He could be normal. But – again, he might not even regain consciousness.' He ran one big hand across his cropped hair, shaking his head. 'Helluva thing, Bren! One *helluva* thing!'

Madigan nodded, his battered face showing nothing.

Parminter lit a cigar, pushing the box across to Madigan who shook his head. He was dizzy enough without the strong tobacco adding to his disorientation.

'There's . . . a background to this you aren't aware of,' the chief marshal said in a more normal tone. 'You know Titus Cattrell's reputation—'

'A hell-raising do-gooder who actually does some good instead of just shouting about it.'

'That'll do – yes. Well, just at the moment he's trying to push through some legislation that's going to put a lot of noses out of joint. Mostly other government officials who have vested interests in big business all across the country, mainly railroads. Cattrell claims the Indians aren't being paid the royalties they're due where the railroad crosses their land. In some cases, they haven't even received the promised settlement money.'

'Indians? Hell, that's a change! Someone going to bat for them.'

'Cattrell wants it made law that they be paid an honest royalty.'

Madigan blew out his cheeks. 'Man, now that will stir up the snakepit!'

'Exactly. Titus has been threatened. There have been two attempts on his life and if it hadn't been for young Kimble, he might be dead right now.'

Madigan frowned. 'I never knew anything about that.'

'No.' Parminter seemed just a little uncomfortable. 'You were on that stolen army payroll assignment halfway across the country. Most field agents were out, too, and the senator needed a bodyguard at once so. . . .'

'You assigned Beau Kimble, not much more than a greenhorn!' Parminter didn't answer and Madigan knew he wasn't about to. A slow smile creased his rugged features. 'But Beau'd fit into the senator's social class, wouldn't he, coming from Virgina aristocracy as he does. And Beau's a presentable young feller, be a fitting escort for Titus's daughter – Emmaline, isn't it? She's round about Beau's age, if I recollect, maybe a little younger.'

'Bren! That's enough! Suffice it to say, Kimble did an admirable job and when we found a tentative link between McLaren and gun-runners and slavers – well, Titus suggested I put Kimble on the case, as a step towards his promotion to full marshal. He was doing very well until—'

'Until his lack of experience showed and McLaren set him up for a killing – and I just happened to be a few miles away, wrapping up my assignment, so you suggested I might like to cover the kid's back.'

'All right, all right – I'll admit I made a mistake

sending in Kimble alone. He lacked experience but there was an urgency. Now . . . well, I was about to say thanks to you, that urgency is taken care of, but you aren't really due any thanks, Bren! No matter your intentions, you still fouled up.'

Madigan waited for it, knowing what was coming, and he wasn't disappointed.

'Titus wants you charged with attempted murder and thrown in jail, but . . . I . . . think I've talked him out of that. But for the moment, you're suspended for two weeks and then – well, he doesn't want you sent on some obscure mission away in the wilderness – he thinks you might very well enjoy that – wants you on hand, right here!' Parminter stabbed an iron finger on to his desk blotter. 'So, you'll be stationed in Washington for a time.'

'How long a time?' Madigan's cracked lips barely moved and his voice was barmy audible, but the thunderous look on his face as he tried to contain the rage welling-up inside him made Parminter ease even further back in his big desk chair.

'Until I say "enough"!' Parminter's voice was harsh and he cleared his throat. 'You should consider your-self lucky you're not behind bars looking at ten years in a penitentiary! Senator Cattrell is out for your blood and I'm doing all I can to keep him away from you, but – you set one foot wrong, Bren, and you're in more trouble than Custer at Little Big Horn.'

Madigan stood, set his battered hat on his head and started for the door. 'I didn't think Cattrell had that much clout.'

Parminter squinted.'Perhaps there's even more

power coming his way. He's transferring to the Diplomatic Corps and, I believe, is aiming for an ambassador's job.'

Madigan shook his head slowly. 'And needs to be seen to be clean and pure – couldn't even risk having a son in the background who might be less than totally intelligent.'

'By God, Bren, you watch your mouth! Where are you going? I haven't finished. . . .'

'I'm going to a place I know down in L Street where a man can relax with perfumed women and silk sheets.'

Parminter shot to his feet, but Madigan was too weary, too disappointed, too frustrated to care, and left the chief marshal's office. 'You must be getting old, if you're letting the strain get to you this way!'

The door closed quietly, but firmly, behind Madigan whose mood didn't improve any when he saw Beaumont T. Kimble sitting in the waiting–room, freshly scrubbed and wearing new clothes, turning a new Stetson slowly between his fingers. He nodded somewhat warily to Madigan. 'How'd things go, Bronco?'

'Ask the chief – we'll compare notes in a couple of weeks – when my suspension's up.'

Kimble felt his face flushing as Madigan went out and left the door partly open behind him. Then Parminter's door opened and the chief marshal beckoned impatiently for Kimble to go in.

That night, Parminter went to see the senator in the big grey building where the man had his office. There

23

was an armed man on the door, another standing in the dimly-lit passage leading to the office. A third man, armed with a sawn-off shotgun as well as twin Colt pistols in soft black-leather holers, nodded politely, said, 'Evenin', Marshal,' and ushered him through the small foyer into Titus Cattrell's inner office.

The senator wasn't a big man, but he gave the impression he was because of his width. He was obviously well fed but looked solid and powerful. His face was square-jawed, his forehead a little lower than a man might expect in someone of his standing, and dark, penetrating eyes glittering beneath bushy, ridged brows. He was working on some papers on a neat, but busy-looking desk, glanced up, eased back in his chair and set down his pen when he saw Parminter.

'Which jail is he in, Miles?'

The marshal sat down in the visitor's chair without being asked, fiddling with his overcoat in his lap. 'I thought we decided against jail, Titus, as being the waste of a good man.'

Cattrell said nothing for a time and Parminter waited, holding the man's angry glare steadily. '*You* decided!'

'He works for me.'

'He shouldn't be working for anybody, goddamnit, after what he did! The man's an irresponsible killer! I know his reputation. If he notched his guns he'd have no butts on the frames!'

'Titus, we've been over all this. It was a genuine mistake. Randy was as good as dead anyway, so Brendan Madigan tried to make the best of a bad deal . . . He's contrite and he did resolve the situation which was about as bad as it gets, you know.'

'Don't take that patronizing attitude with me, Miles! You disappoint me! That's my son in the Washington Hospital, fighting for his life, goddamnit! You expect me to . . . to congratulate the man who made him like that?'

'Of course not – but Madigan's my top man, Titus, and I mean *top man*. It's – it's why young Kimble turned out as well as he has. Oh, he needs a lot more experience, I grant you, but he did save your life twice – and that's thanks to Madigan's training.'

Senator Cattrell was on his feet in an instant, one large fist slamming down on the edge of his desk.'Please spare me this sanctimonious attitude, Miles! The man's a killer! I had his records checked—'

'Damnit, Titus, those records are confidential! You're supposed to make any requests to see them through me! And I sure don't recollect any such request coming from you.'

'I have my own way of working – you know that. Anyway, pettifogging protocol is not an issue as far as I'm concerned. My son's life is – and the life of the man who put him in his present situation.'

Parminter sighed.'I will not lock away such a man as Madigan. I know how hard this must be for you to accept, but *the man did the job he's paid to do in the best way he knew how*. It was a situation that called for split-second judgement, Titus! For God's sake, man, it was a desperate move, but three people had already been shot down in cold blood, only minutes before. It's my conviction that if Madigan hadn't acted when he did, the way he did, Randy and all the others would be dead now. And that includes Madigan and Kimble. Sandy McLaren was a mad dog killer.'

Cattrell's jaw rippled with muscles as he clenched his teeth. 'I don't give a damn about the others!'

'Of course not. I understand that – look, you get on well with Beau Kimble and Emmaline seems to have taken quite a shine to him—'

'She has, but leave her out of this.'

'Kimble was there – he's as horrified as anyone about what happened, but he's most adamant that Madigan did the *only thing he could have*! And he admits that he would not have dared do such a thing himself but, in retrospect, he's *of the opinion that there was no other way.*'

The senator frowned, tapped his fingers against the desk as he walked around it and sat down again in his chair. 'That's Beau's opinion?'

'It is – if you'd like to ask him yourself. . . ?'

'Yes, I'll do that later. All right, Miles, if I'm convinced, what do you intend doing about Madigan? He's not going to waltz out of this smelling of roses – even if Randy recovers. He's not going back to his job as if nothing's happened, Miles, I'm adamant about that.'

'Thought you might be – so I've come up with a plan. Though Madigan won't be happy. . . .'

'I don't give a good goddamn about *his* happiness!'

'Understandable. Well, he'll have to be demoted, and then – God help me! – I'm going to put him on street patrol. Here in Washington.'

Cattrell stared long and hard, thinking about the marshal's words. Then, slowly at first, gradually quickening, a smile stretched out his lips.

'Yes! That will be satisfactory, Miles. *Most satisfactory.*'

That wasn't the reaction Parminter was expecting and he was at a loss for words momentarily as he saw the tight smile now fixed on the senator's face.

'Well – if that's agreeable . . .'

'He serves that two weeks of suspension first without pay – before any other action is taken, Miles, I want that understood.'

The marshal frowned a little and nodded gently. 'Yes, that'll happen. Two weeks' suspension, without pay, a little desk-work, then street patrol.'

'Graveyard shift!'

Parminter hesitated, then nodded. 'All right. We're getting a mite petty now, but I agree.'

'Then we have nothing further to discuss, Miles.' He rang a small silver bell and the door opened immediately and the man with the shotgun and twin Colts in black leather holsters stood there, alert, thumb on the shotgun's hammer spurs. 'Show the marshal out, Tenn, then come back with Corey and Starke.'

Miles Parminter stalked past the guard without even saying goodnight to the senator.

He was piqued and damned if he was going to try to cover it.

CHAPTER 3

COLD SWEAT

They were waiting for him when he turned a corner that led from the residential area of Oregon Avenue through a short, downhill side street to Residency Square.

Madigan still had a mad-on about his punishment.

The two weeks' suspension was nothing, he did it standing on his head as he told a couple of his colleagues over a few drinks.

'I wouldn't mind servin' two weeks suspension in Solomon's!' Clete Hannigan said with a leer. 'Solomon's' was Solomon's Palace, an establishment that catered for men's pleasures, no discrimination, as long as a man had the money to pay. Madigan knew the Madam, Cherry La Rue (real name Addie Pegler) from way back and had often stayed there in the accommodation section free of charge. He had saved Cherry's previous house of pleasure from destruction by fire and nailed the people who were trying to put her out of business. She had never forgotten and, although he didn't take undue advantage of her open invitation to stay at Solomon's whenever he wanted, it was a good retreat after a hard assignment.

Or when other kinds of troubles – like the shooting of Randolph Cattrell – knocked a man's legs from under him.

So the two weeks had passed pleasantly enough and he didn't even miss the money he had been denied. But he was taken aback when Parminter told him he had been demoted from a field agent to Washington Street patrolman.

'That's a goddamn policeman's job, Chief!'

'It's your job until I say different. Dammit, Bren, will you get it through your head that you could be in *jail*! Think yourself lucky you're still walking around free – I've done the best I can here! This is a federal senator, I'm fighting, and he's unforgiving. You know that much about him.'

'Maybe I'll get to know him a little better soon.'

'No you won't! You stay right away from Titus Cattrell! He's got three armed bodyguards and they've been ordered to shoot on sight if you try to approach him!'

Madigan arched his eyebrows.'Kind of prone to over-reaction, this senator, ain't he?'

'It's his son, for God's sake. Randy might be a wild one, but he's Cattrell's *only* son,' Parminter said wearily. 'Look, Bren, you have your orders. The only way you can avoid this is if you resign – now it's up to you.'

Madigan stood slowly, his face bleak, and it gave him a little satisfaction to see the chief marshal make an effort to cover his apprehension.

'I'll resign when *I* say enough,' Madigan said quietly, and turned and walked out of the office.

Parminter released a long breath he hadn't realized he was holding. . . .

Madigan had put in the first week of street patrol and found that, surprisingly, he didn't really mind the chore. It was different, although years ago, he, like every other marshal, had served obligatory time on the streets of Washington before moving on to the more elite section of the marshals, the one they all aspired to – field agent. *Hell, that was a long time ago.*

Still, even though this was punishment, he met a few folk he knew in various parts of the town, was more or less his own boss, although he had strict hours of duty – midnight to dawn, thanks to Cattrell. He even enjoyed the solitude, being essentially a loner. And there had been a little action: a couple of fights to break up and send the drunks on their way with a boot applied to their backsides with varying force; another time he had to move the street-walkers on, at least around the corner and off his beat. He wasn't hard on them: he knew most, knew they needed the money and did no one any real harm. It helped the time pass, anyway.

Of course, there were a few desperate ones who became mixed-up with the fringes of the white-slave trade and the opium dens, but they gave him a wide berth. Only once had he fired a shot, and that had been at a known dealer from way down in Mexico he had spotted, but the man had gotten away. He put in his report and added that it was something that should be followed through, a man like Estrada this far north, in the capital itself. There had to be something important to bring him all the way up here. But he heard nothing further about it.

Then he rounded the corner into the side street leading to Residency Square and suddenly there was a big man stepping out of the shadows, his silhouette showing he wore a gun on each hip and leather gloves that glinted with the dimly reflected light from the square.

Madigan barely had time to note these things when he heard sounds behind and to his left. Two more dark shapes, big men, and, he saw now, wearing bandanna masks over the lower halves of their faces.

No one said anything and the marshal started to reach for his gun but the ones in front and to his left grabbed his attention as they closed in while the man behind clubbed him with a fist to the back of the neck.

It was a stunning blow but slightly off the mark and did not knock him unconscious. He went down to one knee, ears ringing, bright lights wheeling and streaking behind his eyes, and then all three were on to him. Boots thudded into his ribs, fists hammered at his head and upper body. He was rocked and kicked from side to side, but he always fell against one or the other of the attackers. Knees lifted into his face. His head was crushed against a stone wall and consciousness started to slide away rapidly.

Calling on reserves that had been developed over the years, Bronco Madigan thrust his hands against the wall, pushed back and roared to his feet in one sweeping, startling moment. The top of his head – by accident, not design – took one man under the jaw and he heard the teeth clack together like a pistol shot before the man grunted and cursed as he staggered back. Madigan, dizzy and reeling, spun, arms flailing, the back of one fist catching an attacker on the side of the head. The man fell away, trying to keep his balance, and Madigan, panting, turned to meet the third man.

A fist exploded into the middle of his face and he saw a Fourth of July as hard-driven blows hammered at his body.The wall was at his back now and that earlier crack on the head started to affect his senses. He staggered, stumbled forward into another set of hard knuckles that mashed his lips against his teeth. He half straightened and then his legs were kicked from under him and he went down.

It was the worst thing that could have happened and he knew it – briefly, for a split second, before all three of them closed around him, boots swinging brutally, endlessly, into his writhing body. . . .

The world was black with red tinges at the edges. Someone must've placed an empty drum over his head for every sound echoed and throbbed through his aching brain. There must have been a hole in the wall of the drum because he could see something out there, swaying and lurching and jerking as he moved along. . . .

He wasn't doing the moving! Someone was dragging him, heaving him a body-length at a time, breath hissing through pinched nostrils with each effort. Madigan's head and shoulders scraped over cobblestones and he groaned but whoever it was took no notice, kept jerking at him by the legs, pulling him slowly out into misty, pale-yellow light.

He grunted as his legs were dropped and his heels thudded and jarred him clear through to the top of his skull. He groaned again and tried to spit up some blood that was filling his throat.

'Aaaagh! Damn you, Bronco! You spat all over my trousers!'

The voice flitered down, rolling and thrumming around in his head, until something in his aching brain sorted through the words and a vague recognition forced a guttural sound from him.

'B-Beau. . . ? Hell'reyoudoin'here. . . ?'

'Your words are all slurred but I get the lift of your voice so I guess you're asking why I'm here. Was coming to have a talk with you after seeing Emmaline Cattrell home to the senator's town house when I found three men trying to kick you to death in a side street.'

'W-who. . . ?'

'Never mind who! I need to get you into the light so I can see how badly you're hurt . . . I'd say you need to go to the infirmary.'

'No! 'mallri' – had worse'n this . . .'

'Not much, I'll bet, and still managed to get up and walk around!' Then Kimble's vague shape leapt up and he put two fingers in his mouth and whistled shrilly. 'Cabby! Here!'

Madigan vaguely recalled some sort of argument between the cab driver and Kimble, the latter threatening to shoot the man's horse where it stood between the shafts if he didn't help him get Madigan inside the closed cabin.

There was a short time of silence broken by clopping hoofs on cobblestones, a couple of twists and turns, then – a blank space. Until he woke in a narrow infirmary bed with the smell of medicine in his swollen nostrils and Doc Rudd, the official Marshals' medico, on one side with a worried looking Kimble in wrinkled and grubby frock coat and trousers on the other. 'Always said you had a head made of granite, Madigan,' the doctor said, without enthusiasm. 'Beau – you can talk to him but not for too long. I've got more important patients to attend to, so you're on your honour.'

The medico went out and Madigan's blackened swollen eyes followed him. 'Guess he means Randy Cattrell.'

'Well, you seem to be tracking all right!' Kimble sounded surprised, stifled a yawn. 'You've been out for almost twenty-four hours. You must have a bad headache, Bronco.'

'Bad? If I had a *bad* headache I'd be out of here and patrolling the streets. I . . . have . . . the biggest *son-of-a-bitch* of a headache this side of the Rockies!'

'Well, there were three of them – and they were all using their boots, doing their best to kick you to death.'

Madigan rolled his bandaged head slowly on the pillow. 'You . . . drove 'em off?'

'Shouted a lot, ended up putting a couple of shots over their heads but they ran.'

Madigan thought about the young marshal's words. 'Didn't want you to see their faces.'

'They wore bandannas – perhaps you knew them. . . ? I mean, you've made a lot of enemies over the years and it must have seemed like a good opportunity to get you alone on late night patrol.'

'Mebbe. They were careful not to speak, so maybe I might've known them. But most of my enemies would rather shoot me than beat me up.'

'I don't know how you can joke about this! You should see yourself in a mirror.'

'I'll pass – and who's joking?'

Kimble smiled faintly and shook his head.

'I'm obliged, Beau – I likely would be dead by now if you hadn't happened along. . . . No, wait! Recollect you said something about coming looking for me – after taking Emmaline Cattrell home?'

'Yes, we'd been to the theatre. The In-The-Round Shakespearean one – you know the place I mean, on London Terrace? A replica of the original one in England.'

'Know it, but never been there, nor likely to go. You keeping company with Emma Cattrell?'

'Emmaline – the senator likes her to have her full name . . . well, yes, I suppose I am. I got to know her quite well when I was guarding the senator and we attended a few social functions together. Anyway, I knew which shift you were on and I wanted to see how you were—' He stopped, fumbled a little and Madigan helped him out.

'How I was taking my punishment? Well, don't worry, kid, I'm doing all right, actually enjoying it to some extent . . . up till the last patrol, anyway.'

'Well, glad to hear it. I-I thought the chief was being a bit hard, but he was pressured by the senator, and he's one very hard man when he's riled, Bronco.'

Madigan stared at him for a while, his sore eyes beginning to water when he said, 'The chief says you stuck up for me.'

'Not a matter of *sticking-up* for you, you did the only thing you could've – and I told him so, that's all. *I* couldn't've done it but you did and I believe you saved all our lives in the process. I understand perfectly how Senator Cattrell must feel, but the fact remains you did your duty and you did it well. Besides, you saved my life when McLaren set me up. I felt really foolish about that, after all you'd taught me on that first real assignment with Jay Sandlo.'

'We all slip-up occasionally – and you better stop with the flattery, kid, or I'm likely to pull myself up and kiss you.'

Kimble reared back and then grinned widely. 'Thanks for the warning! I'd better be going.' He stifled another yawn. 'I'll look in tomorrow.'

'Won't be here. How's young Cattrell doing, anyway?'

Kimble sobered, lowered his gaze and shook his head briefly. 'Not so good, Bronco, not so good. . . .'

Madigan made no response, merely closed his eyes and lay back on the pillows. He didn't answer when Kimble said his farewells on the way out.

Corey was the bodyguard on the street door of the senator's building and he straightened swiftly, almost jumping up off his seat in surprise when he saw the big figure limping down the street. Corey moved stiffly.

'No need to get up for me, Corey,' Madigan told him coldly as he drew level, stopping and looking at the man, eye to eye. 'You look tired – didn't sleep well last night?'

Corey, a hard-eyed man with thin lips, now stretched these into a razor-line and narrowed his eyes. One was blackened and swollen. 'I slept well enough, Madigan. What happened to you? Get run over by a wagon?'

'Feels about like that,' the marshal admitted, and grabbed the man's hands suddenly, lifting them up for a moment before Corey pulled away, twisting his mouth angrily.

'What the hell you playin' at?'

'Just wanted to feel how soft your hands were. You ought to get a job that gives you more exercise – jumping a man in a dark street won't do nothing for your health.'

'What're you talkin' about. . . ?'

Madigan stabbed two pronged fingers into the man's eyes and, as he reared back, choking a scream of pain, hit him across the stretched throat with the edge of his hand. Corey was still choking and writhing on his way down when the door slammed open and big Starke came rushing out. He took one look at Madigan and Corey, swore, and reached for his six-gun.

Madigan, stiff and aching though he was, stepped forward with a good, speedy movement, snatched the gun from the startled man and slammed him across the side of the head. Starke already had smashed lips and two front teeth missing – and there was a bruise under his jaw where Madigan's head had driven into it accidentally last night. He collapsed without a sound, limbs loose.

Madigan dropped the gun beside him, climbed the short stairway with the aid of the banister and stepped into the small foyer just outside Cattrell's office. Tennery, the guard with the twin Colts in black leather holsters and wearing black gloves on his hands stepped forward instantly, hesitated when he recognized Madigan.

'The hell're you doing here?' the surprised guard said, dropping one hand to a gun butt. 'What're you looking at?'

He asked this last as Madigan twisted his head on his sore and swollen neck, gestured to Tenn's glove.

'Stitching's all split – recent, too, looks like.'

Tennery frowned and looked down at the glove, quickly dropped the hand down to his side where it couldn't be seen. 'So?'

'Just figured you'd like to know – I want to see the senator.'

'No.'

Madigan smiled thinly, splits in his lips cracking open and starting to bleed. 'Yes!'

Tennery started forward, one hand bunching into a big fist. Then Madigan's Colt whispered out of leather and the butt reversed and smashed into the gloved hand. Tenn made a guttural, gagging sound, as bones cracked audibly and he hugged the injured hand to his belly, legs wobbling, looking up at Madigan, face twisted and grey with pain.

As Madigan gunwhipped him to the floor, the office door was wrenched open and Senator Cattrell, face dark with anger, demanded, 'What the hell's going on out here. . . ?' The last word trailed away as he recognized Madigan in his bandages, bruised and torn flesh showing here and there. They had never met in person before but he knew instantly who Madigan was. '*You*!'

'Howdy, Senator. Take a good look. It took your three best men to do this to me. Now all three are out of it and nursing their own injuries.'

Cattrell started to back into his office. 'You touch me and—'

'Not this time – but could come a time, Senator. . . .' There was a movement behind Cattrell and Madigan was surprised to see a young woman he judged to be in her very early twenties, standing beside the senator. She was dressed in a pale-green dress, and her white lace gloves held the silver handle of a parasol. Her face was pale, grey-eyed, the hair showing beneath her bonnet, a deep chestnut.

Madigan guessed she was Emmaline Cattrell, but he shifted his gaze back to the senator who was tight-faced as the girl slipped a gloved hand through the crook of his arm.

'Senator, I just came to tell you I'm truly sorry about your boy. I didn't mean him any harm – I hope he pulls through OK.'

'Apology not accepted!' snapped Cattrell, the girl tugging at his arm. He patted her hand distractedly, glaring at Madigan. '*Not accepted*!'

'Daddy, Beau said Marshal Madigan really is contrite and he—'

'I want no apology from this murdering swine, my dear!'

'Well, it's been delivered and I meant it – but next time, you deliver your own messages to me or I'll send my personal one to you. Might come by .44 calibre express, so it'll be quick, sudden and sure, Senator. Sudden and sure . . . *Adios*. For now.'

Madigan touched his hat brim to the girl and went out smoothly. Senator Cattrell, breathing hard, held onto the office door firmly for a full minute before he allowed the girl to help him across the office to a chair.

He released a shuddering breath and forced a weak smile as he held on briefly to the girl's hand. 'Be a good girl and pour your old man a drink, Emmaline, a very stiff one!'

'Of course, Daddy.' She moved to the sideboy and busied herself with the glasses and the decanter of bourbon. 'I don't blame you for wanting a strong drink, that man is truly frightening!'

Cattrell gulped a big mouthful, not answering.

He had never in his life before this moment had anyone scare him clear down to the marrow in his spine the way Bronco Madigan had just done: he had the senator in complete fear for his life.

Just a few quiet-spoken words and a single look, that was all it took to break him out in a cold sweat. Cattrell emptied his glass and looked at the bottle. The girl made no move to refill the glass. Which was just as well, because one more stiff drink and he would throw-up – that's how shaken he was by Madigan's words.

CHAPTER 4

SPIKED GUNS

Madigan was awakened by a heavy fist pounding on the door of the room he was using in the Federal Barracks. As he was now back on duty – such as it was – he was entitled to living quarters and Parminter would not unbend enough to allow him to stay at Solomon's.

He was stiff and the bruises were more noticeable now; he felt like he had just crawled out from under a stampede of thirsty longhorns sniffing water.

'Who's that hellbent on suicide waking me at this hour! I've just come off duty!'

'Clete Hannigan, Bronco. Ferris is with me.'

Madigan frowned. *What the hell?* Those two weren't noted for their early rising, although, seeing by the clunking old tin alarm clock on the shelf that it was past nine in the morning, he guessed it wasn't all that early to them.

He was yawning when he opened the door, blinking in the bright sunlight streaming into the passage. He frowned when he saw the sober expressions on the faces of Clete and Ferris.

'Who died?' he murmured.

'No one – yet,' Clete Hannigan said and Ferris nudged him, frowning. And for the first time, Madigan began to feel really interested – and maybe just a mite alarmed. 'Chief sent us. Wants to see you in his office right away.'

'What'd he send you two for? Doesn't he figure I can find my way there after all these years?'

'He seems in a real hurry, Bronco,' Fats Ferris said, chewing at his thick lower lip – a habit of his when he was worried. And mostly he was worried.

Madigan shifted his gaze from one to the other, nodded and held the door open. He went to the washstand, poured water from the tin jug into the tin basin and scooped a couple of handfuls over his face, shuddering. He ran wet fingers through his long hair. He was dressed in minutes and when he reached for his gun rig hanging over the back of the chair beside his bed, he found Hannigan already holding it. Bronco arched his eyebrows.

'I'll bring it, *amigo*.'

'The hell you will – I carry my own six-gun.'

'Not this time, Bronco! Hell, don't make it any harder! We got strict orders – and I'm here to tell you, the chief's fit to straighten horseshoes between his teeth.'

Madigan had an inkling of what the trouble could be now and, not wanting to make things worse for the others, nodded and jammed on his hat.

It irked a bit as they walked him across the quadrangle, one each side of him – like he was a prisoner. . . .

They marched him in to Parminter's office and Madigan was surprised to find Titus Cattrell there with Emmaline and another, well-dressed man of about fifty who looked like he had been sucking lemons. Madigan knew him well, one of Washington's top lawyers, Carson Renshaw.

The man's presence, along with the senator and the girl, confirmed Madigan's earlier suspicions.

He was in big trouble.

Parminter, grim as a gravestone, dismissed Clete and Ferris, but told them to wait outside the door. Hannigan was still carrying Madigan's gun rig. Then the chief marshal looked up coldly at Madigan. He spoke formally and bitterly.

'I believe you know everyone here, Marshal Madigan – Lawyer Renshaw has a few words to say.'

Madigan shifted his gaze very slowly to the lawyer who stood from his chair, taking a sheaf of papers from a thin valise. He cleared his throat, adjusted half-moon glasses with gold rims.

'Brendan Lee Madigan, United States Deputy Marshal, it is hereby alleged that you did with intent, assault and cause grievous bodily harm to Wilson Tennery, Lucas Corey and Manfred Starke yesterday whilst on the premises of Senator Titus Cattrell, Constitution Road, East Washington. In addition, you threatened the senator's life on the same premises. You will be required to answer these allegations in a duly convened Court of Justice one week from today. Until such time, you will be retained in custody at the Holding Centre in the cellblock beneath the Justice Building.'

'Hogwash, start to finish, 'Madigan said curtly.

Unperturbed, Renshaw merely gave him a bleak look over the lenses of his glasses and added, 'Do you understand these allegations?'

'I understand someone's got a knot in their rope,' Madigan said harshly and he saw Parminter stir in his chair as if to interrupt, but the chief marshal said nothing, only shot him a warning look. '*I* was the one attacked, two or three nights ago. I went to see the senator to apologize for shooting his son and his bodyguards set on me.'

'Only after you assaulted Mr Corey!' snapped Renshaw, doing all the talking for Cattrell. The girl looked uncomfortable as if she wished she was somewhere else.

Madigan wished *he* was somewhere else.

'Well, I'd had almost two days in the infirmary, twenty-four hours of that in an unconscious state, then I go to the senator's and the first man I see, Corey, shows marks on his face where I knew I hit one of my attackers on the street, while on night patrol.'

'Oh, it was light enough and you had your wits about you sufficiently to know precisely where you struck one of these alleged attackers?'

Renshaw didn't look any too comfortable at the way Madigan stared at him. 'I know where I hit all three – and Corey, Starke and Tennery all had the marks on 'em – just where I put 'em during the fight.'

'So, you're saying these three bodyguards of Senator Cattrell set upon you in the street? Unprovoked. . . ?' Madigan merely continued to stare. 'Or *were they provoked in some way and were merely defending themselves?*'

'Three against one *defending* themselves, Counsellor?' Parminter asked quietly.

But Renshaw was prepared with his answer. 'I would say so. Your man has a certain . . . reputation, Chief Marshall, *as a killer who is not slow to use his gun!* Yes, I would say all three would be within their rights to defend themselves any way they could in such circumstances.'

'Counsellor,' Parminter said sharply. 'This is not a trial! You're acting like you have the full attention of a judge and jury and a courtful of people. You can stop your posturing now – you've read the charges. And you have Judge McGowan's court order for Marshal Madigan to be held in confinement until the trial. Just how you obtained that without Madigan being present or represented is open to debate, but—'

'You are going to comply, I hope, Miles?' Cattrell asked tautly and, at Parminter's curt nod, he smiled triumphantly. 'I warned you not to mess with me, Madigan! Now you face the consequences!'

The girl placed a calming hand on the senator's wrist as his face clouded and he looked at her sharply.

Renshaw interrupted. 'There is no choice. You must comply with Judge McGowan's order, Chief Marshal, which, by the way, was obtained quite

legally, If you wish I can refer you to many prece-
dents. . . .'

Parminter waved a hand irritably. 'I believe you,
Counsellor. You're far too well known for your knowledge of and manipulation of the law for me to even
consider arguing with you.'

'Careful, Chief Marshal! You come dangerously
close to insult and a libel charge!'

Parminter stood, crossed to the door and
motioned in Ferris and Hannigan who both looked
at Madigan. But the man's battered face was unreadable.

'Stand by the prisoner,' Parminter snapped to the
two big officers, and then he turned to Cattrell,
Emmaline and Renshaw. 'If that's all, gentlemen,
and Miss Cattrell. . . ?'

They went out, although Renshaw deliberately
delayed sorting papers into his valise. When the door
had closed behind them Parminter leaned against it.

'You damn fool, Bren! This is something I can't
fight! It's all formally and legally handled by that
snake Renshaw and Cattrell has the wherewithal to
follow it through – what's more, he has the virtuous
Emmaline as a prime witness! She heard you
threaten her father's life! How do you think it's going
to look when *she* takes the stand with her youth and
beauty and air of innocence, folds her hands in her
lap and confirms her father's allegations?'

'I didn't mean it as a threat. It just came out that
way,' Madigan admitted. 'I was riled and wanted to
set Cattrell back on his ass.'

'Well, apparently you succeeded! You frightened

him so much they thought he was having a heart attack and had to call in a doctor – who happens to be brother-in-law to Carson Renshaw and *he* recommended that Cattrell take legal action against you – *and* he has plenty of reason to! Plus the incentive!'

Madigan nodded slowly. 'I guess I was kind of hotheaded in this, but you know me, Chief, I can't abide these fellers who ride a high hoss and figure the shortest way to get where they're going is to trample anyone in their way.'

Parminter sighed and nodded. 'Yes – I know you, Bren! Only too well. But this time you're going to end up in prison if Cattrell has his way! Maybe for years! We have no one on our legal payroll who can beat Renshaw at this kind of game, specially when he's backed by someone like Cattrell!'

'You agreed pretty quick to lock me up till the trial.'

Parminter bristled at Madigan's criticism. 'I did my best! But you know damn well what Renshaw's reputation is! He gets all the I's dotted and T's crossed. You don't have much of a defence! About the only thing you can call on is that twenty-four hours when you were unconscious – it could've affected your thinking. You might be able to claim you weren't thinking straight but that girl will be the clincher, I feel.'

'Maybe I should've resigned when you suggested it.'

'Don't you throw that in my face! Goddammit, Bren, you're a hard son of a bitch! Well, there's nothing more we can do until the trial so you'll just have

47

to make the most of your stay in the holding pens.'

'They call 'em the bullpens' – gonna brand me like a steer? "M" for Marshal, so the other inmates'll know for sure who I am?'

'Bronco's right, Chief,' Clete said suddenly. 'He'll be in there with some fellers he helped put away or kin to men he's killed! He'll be a marked man!'

Parminter's face was bleak. 'Maybe that's something he should've thought about before going off the rails. Now take him down to the Holding Centre! I have a lot to do.'

Madigan, grim-faced, thrust out his hands. Clete and Ferris looked embarrassed and glanced at Parminter who scowled. 'There'll be no need for manacles! Dismissed!'

Hannigan and Ferris were half expecting Madigan to make a break and both wondered if they would shoot at him if he did, but he gave them no trouble. Not that he hadn't thought about running, but his injuries were still giving him hell – that little fracas with Cattrell's bodyguards hadn't done them much good. He was already limping from a damaged cartilage in his right knee and a torn muscle – thanks to someone's boots – in the same thigh.

He knew he wouldn't get far and he didn't want to throw the decision of what to do about an escape attempt onto Clete and Ferris. He had a week before he would go to trial – who knew what might happen in that time?

They would have to transfer him from the bullpens to the court and his injuries would be well on the way to healing by then.

For now he was content to bide his time and even smiled crookedly at Hannigan and Fats Ferris as the turnkey closed the barred door behind him as he entered the holding yard where about nine or ten other prisoners awaiting trial were already gathered, watching his entrance with interest.

A voice from the centre of the cluster said quite clearly, 'Well, looky here! Bronco sonofabitch Madigan! Now ain't this an early Christmas present!'

Beau Kimble was driving a hired fringed surrey when Emmaline told him about her father bringing attempted murder and assault charges against Madigan. She seemed almost glad to bring him such news. He'd noticed she looked strained, almost angry, earlier. Had something happened while he'd been away?

The young marshal had been across to Baltimore in Maryland where his sister was living, now married and with a young babe-in-arms he had never seen, when Madigan had been arrested and thrown into the Holding Centre. He had not yet reported back from his short leave to Marshal Headquarters. Instead, he had called on Emmaline and asked her to go for a drive with him. She agreed readily, but right away he had sensed – *something*, like she'd been *waiting* for him to return. But he didn't aim to spoil things by asking what might be the cause of her tension.

'Oh, it's a lovely afternoon, Beau! Why don't we drive up into the hills? I just love the trees at this time of year.'

Now that was better! Warm smile, enthusiastic – maybe he was imagining things. . . .

Kimble wasn't due to officially return to duty until tomorrow so he agreed, and hired the fringed surrey. They had admired the views from natural rock ledges and were driving down to a wide, clear mountain stream when the girl, who had been silent for some time, suddenly blurted out, 'Your friend Madigan's in jail!'

Kimble hauled rein so suddenly and firmly that the horse reared and pawed the air, whickering. After calming the animal, he hitched around in the seat to face the girl. 'Why?'

Readily enough, she told him, seeing his face harden as she spoke. 'He threatened Daddy! I was there! He knocked out all three bodyguards! He *should* be locked up, Beau! He's dangerous! You must agree!'

'I don't!' he said shortly. 'Your father has overre-acted – as usual.'

The soft look in her eyes hardened. '*As usual?* What does that mean?'

He knew they were going to fight but he made no attempt to tone down his criticisms of the senator. He didn't go into detail, simply named incidents, and each time she drew further away from him. Her jaw jutted in anger.

'How dare you criticize my father this way! After all he's done for you! And *your* father!'

Kimble didn't want to know about that: his father had all kinds of interests and acquaintances, many at government level. He had never approved of such dealings and did his best to avoid knowledge of them. It was the main reason he had refused to go into business with his father.

'Madigan's my friend. He saved my life. I can't – won't – stand by and see him persecuted this way.'

'Persecuted! My Lord, you should have seen his face when he warned my father that his next message to him could well be in the shape of a bullet! He terrified me and he frightened Daddy almost into a heart attack! That's the kind of man you're defending, Beau Kimble! Now, if you would be so kind, I'd like to return home!'

'You wanted to fight, didn't you? All along! I sensed it as soon as we met! What is it I've done now?'

'Take . . . me . . . home!' She wouldn't look at him.

The bumpy ride was made in record time and utter silence. Outside the gates of the Cattrell estate, a footman hurried to help Emmaline down from the buggy. 'Thank you, Beau, for a very illuminating afternoon! Good-*bye*!'

They made no arrangements to meet again and Kimble was in a foul mood when he confronted Parminter and demanded full details of Madigan's incarceration. Surprisingly, the chief marshal gave them to him amiably enough.

'Renshaw's the best there is, Beau. I've racked my brains but I can't see any way that Bren is going to avoid some sort of prison sentence.'

'Nor I, sir,' Kimble muttered, looking at the file Parminter handed him. 'It's probably the tightest corner he's ever been in and we've only got a week to help him.'

Parminter lifted his hard eyes to Kimble's face. 'No "we" don't, Beau. This is none of your concern. You have your job to do.'

'But, sir! I-I'm obligated to help Bronco! I owe him my life! He's taught me so much and although he tends to mock me I know he's sort of proud of me in his own way. I – I don't mean that in any boastful way. . . .'

'I'm sure you don't, Beau, but, as I said, you have your official job to do. A couple of hardcases broke jail a few days ago, Dancey and Barnes. There've been sightings in the Shenandoah Mountains, so they're probably making for the Alleghenies. I want those men brought in, Beau.'

'Sightings? Sir, nine out of ten so-called sightings amount to nothing—'

'Don't try to teach me to suck eggs, Beau! I have reason to believe these sightings are genuine.' He pushed a slim file across the desk, watching his face. 'If they've crossed a state line it's now a federal case. It's all in here. I want you on the trail tomorrow morning.'

Kimble took the file, face sober. 'I'd like to visit Bronco in the bullpens, sir.'

'Not possible.' The chief marshal's tone was clipped. 'We've been advised by our lawyers that it will be best if Madigan doesn't have contact with anyone who might be called as a witness.'

Beau frowned, but nodded gently. Of course: he would be required to take the stand, seeing as he drove off the three men who attacked Madigan. . . .

'Go study that file and get on with your assignment, Beau. I want those two alive if at all possible.'

Kimble left, knowing there was nothing further to discuss. Other marshals knew less than he did but all confirmed Parminter's view that if Kimble was to be a witness, he certainly wouldn't be granted visiting rights.

Annoyed and frustrated, trying to push the inconclusive spat with Emmaline to the back of his mind, Kimble ate a tasteless meal in the canteen and retired to his quarters.

He opened the file Parminter had given him without enthusiasm, but after reading the first page, he sat up, turned up the oil lamp beside his bed and began to read avidly.

'The cunning old so-and-so!' he breathed. 'He'll never admit it, of course, but unless I'm mistaken, he's just shown me how I can help Bronco. . . !'

Maybe, he added silently. Just – *maybe*. If he was wrong – well, Parminter would annihilate him.

But, for Madigan, it was worth the risk.

CHAPTER 5

HIGH MOUNTAIN

The moon came out from behind the clouds just as Kimble eased his mount over the crest. A man not given to cursing, he did say '*Damn!*' with plenty of emphasis, kicked his heels against the claybank's flanks and set it over onto the dark side of the mountain.

He stopped just below the crest, dismounted and took his imported German-made Zeiss field-glasses – a present from his father – from the specially made saddle pouch. They had special lenses for night viewing and he had put them to good use on many occasions.

Tonight was another such time when they proved their worth. He swept them very slowly over the dark, shadow-slashed bulk of the range across from this slope, remembering to keep his elbows tight against his body and to breathe shallowly so as to minimize shakiness.

There was a faint orange point over there that did not move. So it wasn't a firefly – he chuckled slightly: it would have to be a mighty *big* firefly to show up that size in his lenses!

It was the remains of a camp-fire. Kimble shook his head slowly. Unbelievable! Those two amateurs couldn't even hide their camp properly.... He was amazed that they had managed to get this far without being caught. But most of all, he was amazed that they had managed to escape in the first place.

It had come as a surprise to him when he had started to read the file Parminter had given him to learn that the fugitives, Dancey and Barnes, had escaped, not from a prison, as such, but on the way from the Holding Centre to their trial at the Court of Justice.

Parminter had made some written comments in the margins of the file. 'These two aren't noted for their intelligence, Beau, but somehow they chose the only way they could escape at the only possible time they could pull it off; the only way any prisoner could make his break. Study it closely; try to get inside the heads of these two. I think you'll find they must've had outside help. Knowing who or what it was may be of assistance.'

Parminter didn't say just *who* it might be of assistance to, but Beau read between the lines and put Madigan's name in there. Discovering the whys and wherefores would be Kimble's priority once he had captured the men. He never considered that he wouldn't capture them.

And he was right. The fools had only ground-hitched the horses they had stolen from a farm near Mohawk Creek in the foothills of the Shenandoahs, and the young marshal had no trouble in leading both docile animals off into a clump of boulders and weighting their rein ends with a heavy rock.

Then he walked into the camp where the men were snoring loud enough to disturb the crickets whose chirping was sufficient to cover his own approaching footsteps. He prodded one man with the muzzle of his special Mannlicher rifle – another gift from his father, but somewhat changed now since he had joined the Marshals' Service. Madigan had seen to that: he had made Kimble paint over the beautiful hand-fitted silver filigree work, roughed up the silver and gold-inlaid breech plate and generally dulled down the varnish on the chequered inlay on the woodwork. He had also had a telescopic sight made to fit customized clamps on the rifle. Now the sleeping outlaw moaned and muttered something incoherent, turned over irritably. The same thing happened with his companion.

Remembering Madigan's rough methods – not all of which he approved of – in fact only a small percentage met with his approval – Beaumont T. Kimble drew back his boot and planted it heavily against the curved butt of the nearest fugitive. His yell didn't have time to waken his companion because Kimble kicked him also and both sat up, cursing and screwing the sleep from their eyes with dirt-caked hands.

They froze in mid-curse when they saw Kimble covering them with his bolt-action rifle. He kicked a few dry branches on to the glowing coals and the fire flickered into life, spreading its light over the now worried fugitives.

They scrambled to their feet without any coaxing, eyes on the strange-looking rifle. Then they looked at Kimble's young face as the firelight strengthened, exchanged a glance and one of them smirked – Barnes, the vicious one.

'Wipe that grin off your face, Barnes,' Kimble ordered calmly. 'You're welcome to try your luck at jumping me if you want. . . .' The bolt action was a blur as he worked it swiftly and a glittering brass shell danced briefly in the firelight. Before it struck the ground, the bolt slid back home with a solid, oiled snick! that locked another cartridge in the breech. 'There's a box magazine that holds seven shells, gentlemen – six are still in there. If you think maybe I can only shoot at one of you if you leap aside and won't have time to shoot the other, too. . . .' Once again remembering Madigan, he let the sentence drift off and allowed a cold smile to lift one corner of his mouth.

'Who the hell are you?' asked Dancey, the taller, more rawboned of the two. He was unshaven and hatless.

Barnes had a battered hat jammed on a head of long hair which protruded in greasy bunches beneath the brim.

Kimble showed them his badge, told them who he was. They began to look really worried now and stretched their hands a little. 'Keep those fingers together! *Now*!'

'We weren't lookin' to tangle with no federal marshal,' growled Barnes, obeying.

'I expect not – your crime wasn't all that serious, stealing the cash drawer from a gambling saloon. The smart thing to do would've been for you stay for your trial. At worst you'd've only drawn six months.'

'Huh!' scoffed Dancey. 'Mister, we din' have none of that money left! A whore stole it from us before we'd spent more'n a few bucks, but if you reckon Deuce Brannigan would swallow that, you must still believe in fairies!'

'Hell, in jail or not he'd have gotten to us – we just *had* to make a break!' added Barnes. 'So when we got word there was a way out we—'

Dancey kicked his pardner in the ankle. 'Shut up, Andy!'

Kimble eased his hips against a low rock, keeping the men covered, boots sliding a little. 'Now we're getting to the interesting part. Just who helped you make that break?' They stared blankly, defiantly. 'Come on, gentlemen! Everyone knows you don't have enough brains between you to stack a deck of marked cards – *someone* helped you. And I not only want to know who, I want to know *how!*'

'Who you callin' a dummy?' demanded Barnes taking an abrupt and involuntary step forward, his hair-trigger temper driving him to make the move, locked hands starting to come down. Kimble fired, rifle angled upwards slightly, and his hips slid down the low rock at the same time. He had to fight to retain his balance. Barnes screamed. He was lowering his hands from over his head when they jerked as

58

a bullet seared them both.

Barnes staggered and fell to his knees, hugging his bloody hands to his chest. Dancey, who had started to lunge, too, stumbled and fell to *his* knees, hurriedly thrusting his hands high above his head.

'Judas, man, don't shoot! Don't cripple me!'

Kimble was sick at what he had done: it had been an accident – he had meant to fire just above Barnes's head – but he knew Madigan would have approved of the wounding. So he forced his face into hard lines as he worked another shell into the gleaming breech, speaking as coldly as he could.

'All right – we'll deal. Tell me what I want to know and no one else need get hurt!'

'We – we'll tell you!' Dancey almost screamed. 'We'll tell!'

There were two men amongst the ten prisoners in the Holding Centre who hated Madigan's guts with a passion. The man who had called out about an 'early Christmas present' was named Buddy Dean. He was a brutal man, given to using his boots even more than his calloused fists. Inevitably, he had killed a man, kicked him in the head, and the victim happened to have a thin skull and died three days later from a brain haemorrhage.

Madigan had had trouble with Dean before, knew his hang-outs and had tracked him down on one of his night patrols. Within hours, Dean had been in the Holding Centre, awaiting a trial that was due the same day as Madigan's.

To Dean, it really must have seemed like Christmas

when he found Madigan thrown into the prison community with him only a couple of days after his arrival.

It didn't bother Madigan who kept to himself, but one of the other prisoners warned him at the noon meal, the day after his arrival, that Dean had found an ally in a man named Chester and the word was Madigan was due to have an 'accident', possibly fatal.

Madigan thanked the man, name of Yorke, a nervous type up on a charge of beating his wife, desperately contrite now. Some of his so-called friends had spiked his beer at a small birthday party and dumped him at his own door in the early hours of the morning. Naturally, his wife had not been pleased and with the rotgut working in him – he was not normally a man who drank more than a couple of beers at any one time – and after she had struck him for the first time in their married life, he had retaliated with unaccustomed violence and broken her jaw and two ribs. His mother-in-law had brought charges against him and he was terrified about what kind of sentence awaited him.

'First offence shouldn't bring more than a fine,' Madigan had assured him. 'Not if you convince the judge you didn't mean it – and if your wife will have you back.'

'Oh, she says she will,' Yorke had said with vast relief. 'She's as upset as I am, and we've agreed that her mother will have to find someplace else to live. . . .'

Maybe it was because Madigan had given him

some cause for hope, that Yorke brought him the warning.

'I believe that Chester is a-a brutal man. In fact, I've seen him beat up drunks in town.'

'Drunks can't usually fight back,' Madigan said. 'I'm obliged, Yorke.'

It came more quickly than Madigan had expected – and in broad daylight. There was a work-party down behind the main building, stacking logs that were to be used to build a toolshed at some later date. The guards had wandered off around the main building, smoking and yarning. Madigan's eyes narrowed: they were *too* casual about it so he knew they had been bribed to leave the work-party for a time.

He had just resolved to be on the alert when suddenly a rake handle hit him in the back of the legs and they folded under him as he fell awkwardly. The rake's tines sliced at his face and he barely had time to jerk his head aside. The nail-like prongs tore the front of his shirt to shreds and he saw that the rake was being held by Dean.

Madigan's reflexes had always been good and he had had time to recover some more from the beating he had taken at the hands of Cattrell's bodyguards. He snatched the rake handle, pulled hard towards him and Dean stumbled, his grip loosening slightly. Madigan bared his teeth as he thrust back and felt the end of the handle dig deep into Dean's midriff.

The man gagged and went down to his knees, vomiting up his lunch. Madigan clipped him under the jaw with the rake handle and spun as someone yelled a warning – he thought it was Yorke – and

Chester was suddenly upon him. He was a big man, smelling of stale sweat and, strangely, of new-mown grass, and his thick arms encircled Madigan's body before the marshal could bring the rake into play. Chester lifted him effortlessly, swung from the hips, and hurled Madigan against the brick wall.

The marshal bounced off, dazed, and Chester helped Dean to his feet, pushed him towards Madigan.

'Fix 'im!' Chester growled and Dean, gathering his senses now, balled his fists and hammered at the marshal's head and upper body.

Madigan went down – but it was a voluntary move, although Dean thought it was because of his blows. So he moved in, spreading his boots for purchase, preparing to hammer Madigan down into the ground. Still on his side on the gravel, Madigan kicked backwards and his boot heel took Dean in the knee cap. The man howled as it dislocated and he floundered wildly. Madigan clawed one big hand and buried it deep in the man's groin, crushing Dean's genitals. The man choked and danced, his face empurpling as Madigan squeezed brutally, then thrust up and hurled Dean into the path of Chester who was rushing in. The big man fell, instinctively putting out his hands to save himself from injury against the rough bricks of the wall.

Madigan slapped the arms down and Chester grunted as his face crunched into the rough brick-work, scraped down, flesh tearing and bleeding, as he slid to the ground. By then, Madigan had scooped up the forgotten rake, took a grip way back on the handle and swung it two-handed. It hit Chester across the head with such force that the handle splintered. One more whack and the hickory broke clean in two and Chester was away with the fairies and the twittering birds, bleeding from mouth, nose, one eye and both ears.

Dean was no longer interested in anything happening above waist level, but Madigan leaned over him, twisted fingers in his hair, and yanked up his blotchy, pain-contorted face. 'Different when you come up against someone your own size, eh, Dean? Well, you're all through, but this is just to make sure you remember the lesson.'

With what was left of the rake handle, the marshal swung against Dean's head and knocked him into the middle of next week. He threw the shattered hickory away just as the bribed guards came running back, trying to look officious. He saw by their faces they hadn't expected him to be still on his feet. Then looked down at the bloody, prostrate men.

'The hell happened here?' growled the red-haired guard finally, mouth a little open in astonishment.

Madigan shrugged. 'Dunno. They just started fighting each other. Like to've killed themselves if I hadn't taken that rake off 'em.'

He met the guards' looks steadily and when they asked the other prisoners if what Madigan said was true, the men, following Yorke's lead, said that was just the way it happened.

There was little the guards could do except put it into their report that way. Dean and Chester would be glad to admit to a fight between themselves, rather than a murder-attempt on Bronco Madigan.

So the head guard put Dean and Chester into separate cells where they would each stay in solitary confinement until it was time for them to go to trial.

The rest of the prisoners, who had suffered bullying at the hands of Dean and Chester, were mighty friendly to Madigan after that.

The day before they were due to be moved to the Court of Justice cellblock – more heavily guarded than here and in more substantial cells – Yorke came to Madigan during a break in the work of pit-sawing the logs for the new toolshed and said, 'Name Tennery mean anythin' to you, Bronco?'

Madigan stopped rolling a cigarette, looked at Yorke, his expression answer enough. Yorke grinned.

'Uh-huh, I see it does! Well, listen, Bronco, we get to hear all kinds of things in here and we know about your . . . troubles.' Madigan waited, deadpan. 'There's a rumour goin' round that there could be a jailbreak on the court transfer tomorrow. As you're due to be on it, we just wondered, you know? I mean, if there's anythin' we can do to help. . . ?'

Madigan remained deadpan. 'Had a break just before I came here, didn't they? Couple of geniuses named Dancey and Barnes. Too dumb to spring themselves, but my guess is they knew too much and someone didn't want it coming out in court so they broke 'em out, and put a bullet in 'em to make sure.'

Yorke nodded vigorously, impatient for Madigan to finish speaking. 'There was a message for you, too.'

Madigan frowned. 'Message?'

'Yeah! One of the fellers has a sister works in Solomon's Palace – she came to see him yesterday, told him her boss, Cherry La Rue, said a man named Tennery wants to know if you're fit enough to run by now because you're gonna have to pretty soon – that's all.'

'Tennery?' Madigan echoed softly. 'That makes no sense! Only man I know by that name wants to put a bullet in me.' His look sharpened. 'Or is that the idea? Shoot me before I get to court. . . ?' *Was Cherry trying to warn him. . . ?*

Yorke looked worried now. 'Aw, hell, Bronco, I dunno. I-I thought I was bringin' you good news!'

'Well, I'll be ready to run, all right, and it'll have to be fast enough to dodge bullets if Wilson Tennery's gonna be waiting.'

Yorke looked positively miserable. 'I-I'm sure sorry, Bronco! If I'd knowed this Tennery was an enemy of yours – well, I guess you had to be warned, anyway.'

'You did right by telling me, Yorke, but are you sure you got the name right?' Yorke nodded emphatically. 'It sounds like a mix-up to me, but I'll be ready for anything.'

Was someone really going to try and free him tomorrow? Or were they merely setting him up?

To be shot and killed 'while trying to escape'?

CHAPTER 6

FUGITIVE

Yorke's court case had been postponed, because his wife was in the process of dropping charges, having somehow pressured her mother into agreeing to do this. So Yorke had to stay in the Holding Centre until it was finalized and the law decided to turn him loose.

'Bronco, you go careful, man. I been awake most of the night worryin' about what could happen.'

Madigan shook hands briefly, smiling faintly. 'Don't lose any more sleep, Yorke. Whatever's gonna happen will be over in about an hour and I'll either be in the Justice cells or running free.'

Yorke sobered. 'There's a third possibility, Bronco!'

'Yeah, I could be lying dead somewhere between here and the court. But if I am, I'll have some company.'

'Judas, Bronco! Don't it bother you – what might happen?'

'Sure. But till it starts I won't know what I can do about it. That philosophy's gotten me through nigh on twenty years in the Marshals Service, so I'll just stick with it, but I've got a hunch it's all going to work out OK.'

There were five of them on the transfer and the two guards who had been bribed to walk away when Dean and Chester had tried to kill Madigan were the ones riding herd – with sawn-off shotguns.

The bunch of prisoners was shoved and jostled into the back of a wagon that had a rectangular cage of interlaced iron straps fixed to the back. There was a heavy bolt and padlock on the door and the prisoners were in full view all the time. The driver sat alone in the wagon's seat and swore constantly at his team of six mules. The wagon lumbered away from the bullpens and Madigan saw Yorke's pale face at the barred window of his cell. The man waved but Madigan made no move to acknowledge. He rested in a corner, back to the driver, but watching to either side and the rear.

He figured if anything was going to happen, it would be on the short stretch through the woods where the trail from the bullpens curved around a stonemason quarry where stones for the façades of the growing city's new buildings were being measured, trimmed and shaped.

He was right. The armed guards knew this was the best place for an ambush, too, and came alert when two riders appeared at the edge of the trees, keeping to the deep shadows of early morning, but showing enough so that light gleamed on their rifle barrels.

Madigan tensed, aware that none of the other prisoners had seen the riders. But they soon realized something was up when the guards swung their mounts to face the trees, shotguns held in both hands now.

'Driver!' shouted the nearest guard, the one with red hair who seemed to be senior to the other man. 'Whip up your team and get back to the roadway into town pronto!'

The driver, a middle-aged man with big shoulders and thick arms and a cast in one eye, squinted briefly, then cracked his long whip over the mules, standing in his seat to cuss them out imaginatively. The other four prisoners were up on their knees, grasping the iron straps, watching the trees and the guards. The one with the black beard looked over his shoulder at Madigan.

'Better take your boots off so's you can run faster!' He grinned, showing stumps of three or four teeth and Madigan just smiled but made no move. The man frowned, then turned back to see what was happening.

Madigan, though, hitched around so he could watch the driver, just the other side of the iron-lattice wall at his back. The man was still standing, yelling at the mules who were braying and hitting the harness as the lash laid welts across their dusty hides. He was mighty close to the edge and Madigan lunged suddenly, reaching up between the man's spread legs through the gap in the iron straps, grabbing the startled driver by the genitals. The man let out a yell and Madigan pushed hard, straightening his arm.

The driver's scream choked off and he hurtled over the side, whip falling onto the seat, his body bouncing. One of the heavy wagon wheels just missed his legs. The guards were startled and the closest, wild-eyed, spun his mount, lifting his shotgun over the horse's head, calling to the red-haired man who was still watching the riders at the treeline.

Madigan had the whip now, face crushed against the iron straps as he strained to swing it with his arm through the square gap, flicking the lash at the guard now closing in, bringing up his shotgun. The lash struck the man's cheek, laying it open like a rotten orange splitting. He jerked, the shotgun exploding with a roar into the ground. The charge struck close to the man's horse, gravel and maybe a stray ball striking the animal's forelegs. It swerved wildly, hit the side of the wagon, throwing the startled guard against the iron. One of the prisoners, named McKee, grabbed the man around the throat as the man was waving his gun arm wildly.

Madigan strained, reached through and managed to jerk the gun from his grasp. The guard fell off his horse and the red-haired man thundered in, gun to shoulder. The charge would rake the cage and likely everyone in it. Madigan poked the short barrels through and cocked the second hammer, firing instantly.

The redhead yanked back on the reins, pulling his mount up onto its hind legs. The animal took the charge of buckshot in the belly and Madigan swore as it fell, throwing the redhead hard, sending him skidding along the ground.

Then it became a blur of action as the two riders came racing out of the trees and another appeared from the side, angled towards the front. The redhead was up to one knee, lifting his shotgun, when a rider streaked in, leaned out of the saddle and knocked the man unconscious with a blow from his long-barrelled, full-stocked rifle.

Madigan frowned and hardly heard himself murmur in surprise above all the yelling and shouting: '*Kimble, by God*!'

'So you're letting them go,' Madigan said, as he stood smoking by the small camp-fire on the high ridge below the timberline. He was looking across to the spine of the parallel mountain range, briefly seeing the silhouettes of Dancey and Barnes before they dropped below the crest.

'They've earned it – they just stumbled into all of this. And they did help with your break. They'll have a chance this way. As long as Brannigan doesn't catch up with them. No one's quite sure where he is at the moment.'

Madigan drew one last lungful of smoke before flicking his cigarette stub into the fire and turned to the man squatting on a rock nearby holding a tin mug of coffee.

'Hope you're right about 'em, Beau. You're either learning, or Parminter must think you've got more brains than I give you credit for.'

Beaumont T. Kimble smiled. 'Well, *I* thought *you* had more brains, too. You're the only man in the Marshals Service who knows the 'T' in my name stands for Tennyson, yet you didn't figure it out when Cherry sent that message, telling you Mr Tennyson said to get ready for the break.'

'Whore got it wrong – said the message was from a man named Tennery.'

Kimble nodded slowly. 'Ah – I wondered why you never picked-up on the Tennyson. My apologies, Bronco. You are pretty smart after all.'

Madigan nodded, half-smiling. 'Yeah, well, you got me out of that cage, and I'm here now, so someone was pretty smart – but not you! Parminter'll have your scalp for this.'

Kimble shrugged, though his smile had faded some.

'Well, perhaps now we have a little time to ourselves, we should talk things over, Bronco. What d'you say?'

'Let's hear what you've got to say, Beaumont!'

'You know about Dancey and Barnes, stealing the cash box from Deuce Brannigan?'

Madigan nodded. 'How much was in it?' He was a little surprised at the sharp look from Kimble that his question prompted.

'They figured they'd find between five hundred and maybe seven, tops. Big money for them.'

'And. . . ?'

'I think they counted close to the seven, but then a whore managed to steal it from them – this is the cash drawer itself, I'm talking about, a small drawer with a locking lid that fitted inside an ordinary desk drawer. Lovely piece of cabinet-making, hand-rubbed cedar and—'

71

'A cash drawer's a cash drawer no matter what it looks like.'

Kimble smiled. 'Not this one. The whore, in her hurry to hide it on top of her closet in her room at Solomon's, dropped the drawer. It hit on one corner and sprang open, revealing a lower, hidden compartment.'

'How much was in there?' Madigan asked slowly.

Kimble lifted his eye brows. 'One jump ahead as usual, Bronco. It was mostly paper money but some gold pesos, too. Totalling almost twenty-five thousand.'

Madigan was as much impressed as he was surprised. 'So Brannigan's into something else beside cheating other card players . . . gold pesos, you said?'

'In big denominations – as you'd know, very, very few *campesinos* ever get to see money like that, let alone lay their hands on it. Sure not for betting with tinhorns like Brannigan.'

'What I was thinking—' Madigan frowned suddenly and Kimble tensed, waiting for something, but Madigan merely said, 'But Brannigan's got connections – what happened next?'

'The whore – one named Goldie, appropriately enough – d'you know her by the way? Maybe, met her while you were staying at Solomon's?'

'Keep talking, Beau.'

Kimble smiled faintly and nodded. 'Well, Goldie had enough brains to know she had stumbled on something here that was way, way too big for her, so she consulted Cherry La Rue. And Cherry, being the good-hearted soul she is, knew Dancey and Barnes had gotten themselves in a *heap* of trouble.'

Madigan smiled crookedly. 'You're picking up the jargon nicely, Beau. So Cherry arranged to break Dancey and Barnes out so they could get away from Brannigan who was not about to let anyone steal that much money from him.'

'Like I said – one jump ahead. Yes, she arranged to bribe the guards and so on and Dancey and Barnes were – rescued might be a good word.'

'Good as anything else – and what happened? How come they were still around to help you get me away?'

Kimble looked smug. 'We made a deal. Help me and I'd let 'em go. Bronco, the chief gave me the job of bringing in Dancey and Barnes.'

'Federal marshals chasing two-bit thieves like them?' Madigan was genuinely surprised.

'Well, they crossed a state line into North Carolina and made a run for the Shenandoahs before swinging back to the Alleghenies – where I caught up with them.'

'Managed to bust-up Barnes's hands in the process, too. Don't look so worried, Beau. I approve. Seems you're picking up more than just the jargon, eh?'

Kimble was about to protest, tell him it was an accident, but he surprised himself by being pleased with Madigan's approval, even if he hadn't really earned it. Anyway, Barnes's wound was not the issue here.

'Bronco, before I go any further, I have to tell you that Goldie was found floating in the Potomac – with her throat cut.'

Madigan's face was deadpan but Kimble, learning now, watched the eyes and saw that strange veil or dark curtain lower behind them before they glinted briefly. He had seen it before when Madigan was out for revenge at any cost.

'Well, after Goldie was found, Cherry La Rue went to Parminter and explained the whole thing.'

'What happened to the money?'

'I think she turned it over to Parminter who, without actually saying anything, told me how you could escape on your way to the Justice Courts.'

'Parminter *authorized* my escape?'

'Authorized and arranged it – through Cherry, of course. And I'm sure no one would ever be able to trace it back to him. His hint to me was written on the file, but most people wouldn't know what it meant.'

'Well, smoke me! After the way he damn near skinned me alive for shooting young Randy – how's he doing, anyway?'

'Improving. The chief doesn't get along too well with Senator Cattrell, you know, Bronco.'

Madigan grunted. 'And he told you to turn loose Dancey and Barnes?'

'Well – no. That was my own idea. But they're innocent parties in this, Bronco. They're bewildered and scared white.'

'Innocent? They've got an arrest sheet long as my lariat!' He shrugged. 'But they're small change, and I guess they paid their way – told you who to bribe and so on?'

'Yes. Bronco, Parminter doesn't want to see you, as you'll understand, you being officially a fugitive now, but he's got an assignment for you.'

Madigan laughed briefly. 'Well, it won't be the first time I've gone undercover, but this is the first time when I'm really a fugitive. What's the assignment?'

Kimble was sober now, looking off across the blue haze that was faintly blurring the outline of the far range where Dancey and Barnes had disappeared. 'Felipe Estrada.'

Madigan stood so fast he almost slipped as he straightened beside his rock. Frown lines dug deep into the weathered flesh of his forehead, like old scars from a puma's claws.

'Estrada! I saw him one night on street patrol, down L Street. I told Parminter about it, put in a report that maybe he should be checked out, because his usual stamping-ground is along the Rio ... though I once heard he had done some business in person in Santa Fe. Washington's a long ways north for him. But Parminter never followed through. . . .' He let the words trail off. 'God, he plays things close to his chest! He must've known about Estrada being up here even before I accidentally spotted him! Likely already had him under surveillance.'

'You're probably right – he didn't mention that, but he wants you to find out what Estrada was doing up here and who he saw and, of course, every detail you can dig up.'

'Hell, I'll have to hang around Washington to do that! I'm bound to be spotted.'

'I could do that part – with your guidance, of course.'

Madigan's frown deepened and he looked suddenly wary. 'You could? Your part's finished, isn't it?'

Kimble was smiling like a cat with a bellyful of cream. 'Forgot to mention that we'll be working on this together, Bronco – I'm your sidekick again.'

Madigan only said one word, but it was mightily descriptive of his feelings about having to work side by side with young Beaumont T. Kimble again.

The young marshal looked genuinely hurt.

CHAPTER 7

PARDS!

Cherry La Rue had been a fine-looking woman in her youth and could still turn plenty of heads when she walked down the street or swayed into a ballroom on the arm of some rich man who paid her to act as his companion at one of the many Washington society functions.

Everyone knew who she was and what her business was – at least the Solomon's Palace part: there were many levels of other businesses that held her attention and helped swell her coffers – and almost every woman was jealous, even though their tongues were not kind when they spoke of her.

She must have been pushing 50 but had the figure of a 30 year old who had taken care of her body. She wore a minimum of make-up, kept her naturally blonde hair upswept and held in place with an old-fashioned rhinestone-and-jet clasp that had belonged to her mother: a small piece of sentimentality. Her clothes were of excellent quality, shipped in from Paris, London and Cairo. Her perfumes were subtle and conjured up visions (if not fantasies) of exotic harems. The only word to describe her jewellery was 'magnificent'.

Madigan walked into her apartment that was decorated in the ways of the Orient and the spice-laden East, nodded to a man who sat at a tiny desk in a small, half-hidden alcove. He wasn't a big man, and his clothes were neat but nothing out of the ordinary. He was well-enough groomed and nodded back to Madigan, allowing his right hand to slide back from the cocked six-gun clipped beneath the desk.

'Still awake, Frenchy?'

'Enough to see you, Madigan.'

The fugitive marshal smiled thinly, crossed the room to where Cherry La Rue was just pouring a fine porcelain *demitasse* to accompany her own.

'I was expecting you before this, Bren,' she said, smiling, eyes affectionate as she watched the battered marshal sit down and pick up the small cup.

'Can never get my fingers through these damn small handles,' he complained, sipping gingerly.

'Just don't break it off, please! – I take it you weren't seen coming here?' He gave her a look and she swiftly held up her hand. 'I'm sorry – I should know better than to ask – I won't keep you as you are officially on the run. What do you want to know?'

'About Estrada.'

Her rouged lips curled. 'An unlikeable little man. Convinced he's God's gift to women – but my girls would dispute that! I don't know much about his visit to Washington, except I hear he came to contact some of the men who back his . . . interests, mostly south of the Rio.'

'They're the men I'm interested in, Cherry. Can you give me a list?'

Her slanted green eyes studied him closely. 'You should know better than to ask, Brendan!'

'Estrada's a son of a bitch who needs burying. He's thumbed his nose at us for years from south of the Rio. Now that something has driven him this far north, we have to grab the chance – you can see that.' She remained silent. 'Just what is it that's brought him here, Cherry? C'mon! I'm on the run and I don't have much time. Something mighty important has brought that snake all the way up here.'

His face was as hard as Cherry La Rue had ever seen it and there was a flutter in her stomach that betrayed her feelings in the trembling of her hand as she set down her *demitasse*, rattling it against its tiny saucer.

'Brendan, you know I don't care for this kind of approach! Most unsubtle and – well, disrespectful.'

'It's me, Addie. What you see is what you get.'

Her pale face was suddenly tight. 'So! This is the way it's going to be? Rough and ready. . . ?'

'Just giving you a small reminder of our roots. Neither of us would be where we are – wherever *that* is – if we hadn't been tough.'

Her expression didn't change, then after a small frown, she smiled with white teeth that had cost a small fortune to make that way after many visits to Europe. 'Straight from the shoulder as usual, Bren!

But you're asking a lot – far too much, really – but, for old times' sake, I can tell you that Estrada dare not return to Mexico.'

Madigan eased forward, alert, intent.

'I have no details, only the sketchiest outline. Something to do with a young – very young – niece of *El Presidente* himself.'

Madigan whistled soundlessly with his healing lips. 'So, Estrada's been thinking below his belt again. Was always his weakness, how he got into the white slavery thing in the first place. That bastard's caused more misery and death than *El Presidente* himself, and they say he climbed over mountains of bodies to get where he is. . . .'

'As I said, I know no details. I'm not even sure if this is his real reason for being here, but it's all I can – or am willing – to tell you. You understand: if I'm to continue my business in its present state, I have to demonstrate my discretion constantly and my ability to keep secrets.'

'Sure, and my business depends on me finding out secrets people like you try to keep from me.' His voice was cold.

She looked past his shoulder and smiled slightly. 'It's all right, Frenchy. Go back to your station.'

Madigan didn't bother looking around: he knew Frenchy was merely doing his job, watching out for Cherry.

'Another angle for you to think about, Cherry – Goldie.' She straightened slightly. 'She was a strange kid. Likely was attracted to that cash drawer for its looks, more than what was in it. I hear it was polished, attractive.'

'She did like nice things.' Her voice was low and husky now, sad. 'That drawer was very well made, from some old desk, I hear. *That's* what would've held her interest, although she would know so much money meant trouble for someone.'

She looked directly at the lawman, eyes narrowed. 'But those bastards made no allowance for her mental deficiencies, just – cut her throat and dumped her like so much dead meat!'

It wasn't often that Madigan saw Addie Pegler showing emotion about one of her employees who had met such a fate. . . . He had her riled now, and in the right direction.

'They're the bastards I'm after, Cherry,' he said softly. 'You can bet Estrada's in this somewhere . . . I still need the names of the people he came to see in Washington.'

He knew it wasn't fear in her eyes, but there was a sudden and acute wariness as she looked at him, averted her gaze, then sighed.

'All I can say is that I did hear that Estrada saw a couple of senators before he left town: the word is he's going to Missouri – I have no idea why, but another source claims he's stopping off in Lexington, Kentucky.'

'Well, it's good of Estrada to leave such an easy trail for us to follow. If your info is right, that's fine, but I wouldn't want to find it was just a way of getting rid of me right now—'

She slammed her cup down so hard on to the saucer that it cracked and she shot Madigan a

81

venomous look. 'Now see what you've made me do! Damn you, Bren Madigan!'

Frenchy appeared at the doorway of his alcove, one hand behind his back. 'Will I show him out, Cherry?'

'Yes!'

Madigan knew when he had outstayed his welcome – besides, he had learned more than he had expected. He nodded to them both and left, wondering if Kimble had managed to trace Deuce Brannigan who seemed to have disappeared into thin air.

The thought was still forming in his head when he heard the crash of gunfire.

It came from the street behind this one where he now stood – the noisy street they called Drunkard's Row because of all the saloons there.

Brannigan had had the gambling concession in one of them . . . The AcesHi.

Bronco Madigan sprinted down to the intersection. When he came to Drunkard's Row he saw the trouble was outside the AcesHi saloon – outside or inside? At least the gawkers were gathered around the etched glass doors jostling to see, but some were scattering and running for the alley mouth that ran down the right side of the building.

Madigan knew his way around this area and dodged into an evil-smelling lane, groped his way down and tripped over some rubbish, but saved himself from falling all the way. Stumbling, he skirted the dark building, found a gap in the high fence that separated it from the saloon. He ducked instinctively as two guns crashed close by and a man grunted and there were clattering sounds. Crouching, Madigan saw a body tumbling down the outside stairway at the back of the AcesHi.

'I hope that's not you, Kimble!' he said quietly, and jumped as a voice spoke only a few feet away from the darkness on his right.

'Didn't know you cared, Bronco. No, that's one of Brannigan's friends. He was waiting to ambush me but I caught a glimpse of light on his gun up there on the landing.'

Well, Kimble always did have good eyesight and powers of observation but – 'Brannigan? Is he still hanging around these parts?'

'Seems so. I picked up a hint and went after him. He came at me with a blazing gun. I think I winged him but he got away by jumping through a window on to a waiting horse. This feller I just shot was waiting to cover his back.'

Madigan knelt by the crumpled man at the foot of the stairs as some of the gawkers came crowding in tentatively. He looked up, keeping his face in shadow – he was still a 'wanted' man as far as folk here knew, and he hadn't been popular in Drunkard's Row.

'Better get a sawbones,' he snapped in a deeper-than-usual voice. 'Now! Clear these men away from here, Deputy!'

He snapped this last to Kimble who, a little surprised, pushed the men back up the alley and repeated Madigan's order for someone to fetch a sawbones.

Bronco, meantime, shook the wounded man and

saw his dulled eyes flicker open in reflected light. 'Casey, you're hit pretty bad, but you could pull through if a sawbones gets here pronto. Thing is, depends what condition he finds you in. As you are, OK, you're in for a lot of pain and time in the infirmary, but he could find you in such a bad way that you'll be in for a lot more pain – and might never come out of the infirmary – except in a coffin. Or, if you're lucky, a wheel chair, but maybe that wouldn't be so lucky . . . What d'you say, Case. . . ?'

When Kimble came back and knelt beside Madigan and the wounded man, he asked, 'How bad's he hit?'

'Think you might've lung-shot him. Don't worry about him – Casey's no loss.'

'Wh-what're you saying? Is he already dead?'

'Not quite. Told me something interesting, though, Brannigan's making for Kentucky after he catches up with Dancey and Barnes. Cherry said Estrada's heading that way, too.'

'Well, that's not good news!'

'Not for Dancey and Barnes. But don't let's waste time – go fetch our horses and let's get after Brannigan.'

Kimble rose and turned away, then swung back.

'Casey seems to be in far worse condition than when you sent me to get rid of those gawkers . . .'

'Yeah. Deteriorating fast – but he did the right thing and told us what we wanted to know.'

'Told you, you mean?'

'Yeah, but I'm a generous soul, Beaumont, I'll share my info with you. Now don't waste any more

84

time. Brannigan's burning the breeze.'

They rode through most of the night then holed-up for a rest in a heavily timbered hollow by a stream. Madigan crouched by the small fire, frying sowbelly with some crumbled stale biscuits, tossing in some wild onions for flavour. It smelled mighty good and Kimble waited impatiently, preparing the coffee pot as he did so.

He gave the fugitive marshal a few strange looks – which Madigan noticed though gave no sign that he had – and he knew Kimble was still worrying over Casey's condition. He was shaping-up as a reasonable marshal, was Beau, but he still had too many soft spots, too many noble ideas that might even get him killed unless he toughened-up and made himself a damn sight more ruthless than he was at present.

'How can you be so sure Dancey and Barnes will come this way?' Kimble asked abruptly, as Madigan slapped spoonfuls of the cooked mush on to two battered tin platters. He shoved one in Kimble's direction, tossed him a fork with bent tines and picked up his own platter, eating immediately.

'Dunno which trail they might take – they been on the run in this neck of the woods for so long they'd know plenty I ain't never seen.'

'Then – you're taking pot-luck?'

'Groping in the dark'd be closer to it.'

Kimble paused in chewing his food – which he liked: surpringly enough, it tasted as good as it had smelled while being cooked. 'Well, surely that's not good enough, Bronco!'

Madigan seemed genuinely surprised. 'No? Why?'

'Well, I mean, if we're just . . . wandering blindly, it means Brannigan's likely to catch up with Dancey and Barnes and kill them before we arrive.'

Madigan shrugged. 'They knew the risks when they stole money from a bad-ass like Brannigan.'

'But – they helped us, Bronco! They even helped rescue you from that prison wagon, told us what they knew—'

'And why'd they do that? To save their own skins.'

'Well, they're hardly top-of-the-list fugitives! No ten-thousand-dollar reward on their heads! In fact, I consider them pretty much harmless, just a little rough and wild – reckless, even stupid, if you like. . . .'

Madigan nodded. 'I'll go along with that.'

Kimble frowned. 'But this way, you're gambling with their lives! Brannigan'll kill them, there's no doubt about that. He won't let them get away with stealing from him, whether it was twenty-five dollars or twenty-five thousand! He's mean and vindictive, and, seems to me, if he's mixed up with Estrada, far more of a menace to society than Dancey and Barnes!'

'Sure, that's why I'm concentrating on him.'

'You call this "concentrating"? Just heading in the general direction you *think* Dancey and Barnes may've taken?'

Madigan sighed, set down his plate, started to pour coffee but saw it wasn't yet ready. He replaced the pot on the fire with an oath as he burned his fingers, started to build a cigarette.

'I dunno whether Dancey and Barnes came this

way or not, Beau, but *Brannigan* did. We're following his trail.'

'How can you possibly tell? You know I'm pretty good at finding trail sign, but I've seen nothing to make me think Brannigan came this way.'

Madigan sighed again. 'God, kid, I'm bone weary and I'm tired of having to explain every goddamn thing to you. Try using your head for once – Brannigan quit town in the dark, with your lead whistling about his ears and maybe one of your bullets under his hide. He had his horse waiting which means he'd have grub and water and ammo. So he'll take the shortest trail leading south-west into Kentucky – right?'

'Oh, now I see – we go all out to catch up with Brannigan before he reaches the other two.'

'Not necessarily.' Madigan shook his head slowly and lit his smoke, exhaled towards the angry-looking Kimble. 'If he gets there first, we're close enough to hear any shooting and we close in and we'll nail us Brannigan – because neither Dancey nor Barnes are good enough to beat him.'

'My God! You're just using them as bait!'

'Well, hell, sure I am! If you'd just shake them patty-cake ideas you still have about fair play, you'd've seen right off it's the only way. You cut down their odds a bit by shooting Barnes in the hands. Now I'm not complaining; it's good to see you can be a little ruthless when you have to. . . .'

He stopped because he thought Kimble was going to say something about that, but the man subsided and Madigan continued, ' 'Sides, Dancey and Barnes *might* survive. In which case, no harm done.'

Beaumont T. Kimble shook his head slowly and with not a little disgust showing on his taut face.

'I thought we were going to work together on this, Bronco! Do things properly, share ideas, talk them out before we rushed into anything. . . ?'

'Chris'sakes, kid, snap out of it! You've done OK on your assignments so far – yeah, with a little help, sure, here and there, but, in general, you've shown you've got what it takes to make a pretty good marshal. Senator Sandlo had no complaints about your bodyguard work, even if he did turn out to be the villain of the piece. But you have to be harder, Beau. And I mean *all* the time. Shooting Barnes to show you weren't in no mood for playing games, was a good move and it got him talking, but you have to be prepared to do that and a lot worse if you're gonna be a successful marshal.'

'Just like you?' There was bitterness in Kimble's tone and Madigan frowned slightly, answering curtly.

'Be your own man, kid. You don't have to copy anybody in the long run. Do things your way, then you've got only yourself to blame if it gets you killed.'

He finished his smoke while Kimble sat there in tight-lipped silence, then reached for the coffee pot and poured the black, steaming liquid into the two tin mugs. He handed one to Kimble.

'Bronco, it was an accident.'

Madigan frowned. 'What was?'

'My shooting Barnes – in the hands. I fell, the gun went off and shot lower then I meant. Barnes' hands were in the way . . . I – wasn't being tough or ruthless.

I . . . made a mistake.'

'Well, we can all make mistakes.' Madigan watched him closely. 'But you had enough sense to let him think you were ready to cripple him to make him talk . . . that's a step in the right direction.'

Kimble scowled – he didn't really want to think about that. He sat there tight-lipped, holding his coffee.

'Come on, Beau, drink up. Then we'll catch a couple of hours' sleep and get moving by sun-up. Ought to have Brannigan in our sights before we reach Warm Springs.'

'What're we going to do first? Shoot Brannigan – or bury Dancey and Barnes?' the young marshal asked, bitterly.

Madigan smiled crookedly. 'I'll leave the choice to you, *pard*. Don't matter to me one way or t'other.'

CHAPTER 8

RIDERS WEST

One thing about Beaumont T. Kimble: he could react surly and hurt in a child-like manner after having a strip torn off him for making a mistake, but he recovered pretty fast. He didn't seem to hold a grudge. Which was a good thing.

Madigan had noticed it on the first assignment they had shared, riding-herd on a Senator Jay Sandlo who, knowing Kimble's father, had exploited the young green marshal in an effort to cover-up his own lawless failings. In the end, Kimble had been instrumental in killing Sandlo and virtually saving Madigan's life.

Openly, that kind of thing cut no ice with Brendan 'Bronco' Madigan – he figured it was any marshal's duty to protect his pard, but inwardly, he was a man who could never forget such a thing. He had Kimble's future welfare in the Marshals' Service at heart and if he had to hammer the kid down and make him eat crow to get a point across, then he would do it.

It didn't matter to Madigan if the kid ended up hating his guts, as long as Kimble learned his lessons well. At the same time, he was pleased when Kimble soon shook his hostility when it was time to break camp, even offering Madigan some sweetmeats from a wrapped package he took from his saddle-bags.

'What's this?'

Kimble looked slightly embarrassed. 'Home-made chocolate with nuts and raisins and such things.'

Madigan arched his eyebrows as he took a bite: he was kind of partial to chocolate studded with fruit and nuts. 'You made this?'

'No, no – Emmaline Cattrell. Some paid-companion of a visitor to the senator got bored waiting for her escort and showed Em how. She was quite proud of her achievement – but since then we've had a . . . falling-out.'

Madigan spoke with his mouth full. 'Last time I had these was in Mexico – serious falling-out?'

He thought Kimble wasn't going to answer but by the time they had mounted and started down into the valley between the ranges, Kimble said, 'Could be serious. She felt I'd insulted her father. Kind of hinted he hadn't done much for his good image by setting his guards on you. . . .'

Madigan pursed his lips. 'Well, it's a point whether he did that, or they acted on their own. Wilson Tennery has never seen eye to eye with me and the others follow his lead.'

'Well, I thought it was worth debating but—' He

shrugged. 'She was in a strange mood, seemed to almost want a fight. I'll have to try and square things when I get back.'

Madigan said nothing: obviously Kimble didn't realize just what a dangerous assignment they were on. He had had dealings with Felipe Estrada only once, south of the Border, on the man's own stamping ground, and Madigan had been lucky to get away with his life. Estrada wasn't the kind of man to worry about international boundaries or the laws of any country, his own or someone else's. Madigan couldn't shake the feeling that the fact that Estrada travelled this far north pointed up just how important the deal was – whatever it was he was working on.

The Mexican had always been ruthless, a bandido leader and *rebelde* – wherever he saw the chance for a fast buck. Morals or legality were never considerations with Estrada. Any obstacles were easily taken care of – a bribe if necessary, a bullet preferred. Such tactics appealed to some of the men who were planning on taking over the government of Mexico and Estrada found himself in exalted company, helping these men into positions of power, and thereby benefiting himself once they were there.

In Mexico, Estrada kept a low profile, but he was a mighty powerful and influential man, had strong backing, and a deadly gunfighter companion known as *El Halcon*, The Hawk.

Parminter, bound by codes and laws that had never much bothered Madigan, had to step easy. Which was why, on the surface, Madigan's first report about the sighting of Estrada in Washington had nothing officially done about it – Parminter had relegated it to a 'Developments Pending' file which kept it open but without any action having to be taken 'for the moment'.

It smelled to Madigan as if Estrada might have some inroads into the US Government that would protect him up here. Not a good thought but entirely possible. For someone like Kimble, it would be an insurmountable stumbling block. For someone like Madigan – hell, it was no more than a challenge.

If he couldn't find a way around it, there was always a bullet waiting – somewhere – with Estrada's name on it. He figured he could locate that particular bullet if it became necessary.

But he mentioned none of this to Kimble: no use throwing the young marshal into a tizzy, not with his concept of right and wrong and what was lawful: he was a natural worrier, anyway. Look at him now, gnawing his fingernails, no doubt thinking of Emmaline and her childish moods. . . .

They were still in Virginia when they came down out of the mountains into the wide, long and beautiful Shenandoah Valley. It was different to riding through the frontier west, Madigan couldn't help but notice, as he had on other occasions when working up here.

There were signs of habitation everywhere: farms and small settlements, permanent-looking road signs, several riders or families in wagons or carts taking produce to nearby towns. The roads themselves were just that – 'roads', wider, showing signs of more-or-less regular upkeep, having more purpose to their direction, not wandering all over the country side like rutted, narrow western trails.

There were signs of civilization everywhere.

Most folk were friendly, gave a wave, or shouted a greeting as they passed on the trails.

'We headed right for Warm Springs?' Madigan called to one family group riding a flatbed wagon loaded with fresh produce. He knew they were on the right trail, but he wanted to open a brief conversation.

'You're on the right road, friend,' the man answered, lanky and sunburned, wearing home-made shirt and leather breeches that were getting a mite tight across his midriff. 'Take the next fork left.'

'Obliged, *amigo*. We're kind of out of our depth up here. Come from way south—'

'I noticed your accent and use of the word *amigo*. Means friend, doesn't it?'

'Sure does. Friend of ours, a Mexican, matter of fact, was heading this way. Maybe on the stage or with a few friends riding in company – you wouldn't've seen him, at all?'

The man held a brief conference with his wife whose face was hidden by the shadow of a stovepipe bonnet, and then one of the girls in blonde pigtails kept shaking her father's shoulder until he rounded on her with mild anger. She spoke behind a hand raised to her face, big blue eyes turned in Madigan and Kimble's direction.

The man cleared his throat. 'Friend, my daughter, Angelina, says she saw a small bunch of riders flanking a black private-style coach yesterday. It was such

94

an unusual sight out here that she left her chores to run to a ridge to watch. Two men wearing what she took to be Spanish clothing, stepped down from the coach to stretch their legs at the stream, while the horses watered. She isn't sure, but she thinks they took the west fork – which would be in the direction of Warm Springs.'

'I *am* sure, Father!' the girl said abruptly, looking directly at Kimble now, smiling tentatively. 'Your Mexican friend did take the Warm Springs trail, mister.'

The woman pulled the girl back down to her seat and the man frowned admonishingly at her.

'Obliged, miss,' Madigan said, touching a hand to his hatbrim. 'Ride well, *amigos*.'

They drove by and Kimble could feel the blonde girl's stare on his back. 'She still watching me?'

'Eating you up, Beau. Well, we're on the right trail. Have to get some more speed out of these broncs, though.'

'What about Dancey and Barnes? We – you never even asked about them.'

'Told you, they're not important, except to draw Estrada. Sounds like he's got his own bodyguards along, including *El Halcon*. Better clean that Mannlicher when you get a chance, Beau. Clean it and load it fully. Put on your telescopic sight if you want.'

'Wait up, Bronco! It looks to me like Estrada has some sort of official backing, riding in a hired coach, with outriders guarding him! I mean, that's "official" kind of treatment. We better sniff out the situation very carefully before we go helling-in with guns blazing.'

Madigan smiled. 'You're beginning to sound like one of us, Beau. Better do some work on *thinking* like a marshal, too, though.'

'I-I thought I was! Being circumspect, careful not to upset any offical situation. I mean, it's obvious that Estrada is travelling these back roads so he won't be seen.'

'Sure. The sneaky bastard's up to something, that's what.'

'But how do you know, Bronco? I-I'm trying to work out the way you approach these things but – well, your methods don't seem to be in the *Marshals' Manual* or *Code Of Conduct*!'

'My methods get results, kid, that's what counts.'

'I'm not so sure. It's my opinion that Parminter covers for you a lot, because of your war service maybe, or for some other reason. But I've seen him suspend some men who've stepped away from the official line far less seriously than you do at times.'

Madigan smiled. 'Kid, you're more observant than I figured!' That was his only comment.

Then they spurred their mounts along the road, came to the fork, and swung into the west arm.

Kimble still looked worried as their mounts lifted a trail of dust behind them.

They were in a ravine, making their way along a narrow, winding trail, when they heard distant gunfire.

Pausing to listen for a few minutes, Madigan

glanced at Kimble. 'Six-gun, rifle and shotgun. Who you figure?'

Kimble's mouth was a tight, thin line. 'Has to be Brannigan – and Dancey and Barnes. He used a sawn-off shotgun with the trigger-guard removed so he could shoot more easily with the bandages on his hands when we got you away.'

'Let's go see.'

It was still early afternoon but the shadows were thick and heavy down in the ravine, the high sides seeming to lean out across the sky, leaving a ragged slash in the blue. Madigan led but he hadn't yet unshipped his rifle. Kimble had his Mannlicher across his thighs, held there by his right hand. The bolt action was closed so Madigan knew there was already a cartridge in the breech. He nodded in satisfaction: Beau was getting the message, riding in to possible danger as well prepared as he could be. *But he still seemed edgy. Something on his mind. Maybe the damn girl. . . .*

He had turned out pretty damn good on that last case they had worked together – well, it was the first shared assignment as well – but he seemed to have either forgotten some of what he had been taught or else the old 'fair-play' notion had been stronger than Madigan figured. The kid was hesitant, but only because he wanted to see fairness done – not possible in many situations they came across. Beau was going to have to learn that bit all over again.

Well, no time to worry about such things now: they had cleared the ravine and without the deadening effect of the heavy vegetation, the sounds of shooting were much louder.

'That's coming from just over yonder ridge!' Madigan snapped, sliding his battered Winchester out of the saddle scabbard now.

He spurred away and Kimble raced his mount after him, calling, 'Bronco! We need them all alive for best results!'

Bronco Madigan didn't reply or give any sign that he had heard. They topped-out on the rise in a cloud of dust and gravel and both hauled reins together, looking down at the scene before them.

It was Deuce Brannigan, all right, and he was the one with a rifle, stretched out amongst some rocks on his belly, canteen beside him, open box of ammunition ready for a long siege if necessary.

Below him again on a grassy bench dotted with rocks and deadfalls, were two men: Dancey and Barnes, the latter easily recognizable by the white, though grubby and ragged, bandages on his hands. He was lying on his belly, his shotgun, broken for reloading, a yard from his hand. His hat was askew and there were a couple of dark stains showing on his shirt.

'Looks like he's killed Barnes!' Kimble allowed, but Madigan didn't answer: he wasn't a man who went in much for stating the obvious.

He levered a shell into the Winchester and without saying anything, slid from the saddle, ran to a flat rock over the ridge crest and dropped to one knee. The Winchester thundered and whiplashed in three fast shots. First Brannigan's canteen leapt into the air, trailing precious water from the jagged hole torn in the cloth-covered metal. The next shot smashed into the open box of cartridges and they seemed to leap up in a glittering, brassy fan, causing Brannigan to heave away on to his side, one arm protectively across his face. But none of them exploded and Madigan's third shot slammed into the big gambler and knocked him flat. Kimble spurred his mount past Madigan, over the crest, sliding and weaving down the slope, reins between his teeth, the Mannlicher lifting.

Brannigan was hit badly and fought to raise his own rifle but Kimble fired, the shot ricocheting from the rock beside the man.

'Give up, Brannigan! We've got you cornered!'

'*Christ!*' hissed Madigan, leaping to his feet and running down the slope, twisting to the side so he could slide with more control. 'Get away from him, Beau!' he shouted, as Brannigan's rifle came around, even as Kimble worked the bolt on the Mannlicher.

Kimble, fighting the horse's wild descent as well as trying to reload the rifle, fumbled, and Brannigan triggered. Kimble's sorrel shuddered and turned sideways, felt the edge of the small ledge crumble beneath it. The head came around, eyes wild and staring, saliva streaming from the open mouth, threads of mucus from the flared nostrils, and animal and rider started to go down. Dust boiled and Kimble kicked free of the stirrups and jumped, sprawling and sliding.

Madigan passed him, skidding to a stop on a flat section, Winchester butt braced into his hip. He triggered and levered twice and when the dust and powdersmoke cleared, Brannigan lay in an awkwardly twisted heap, sprawled amongst the rocks he had used for protection.

Madigan leapt past him, spun towards Dancey who was leaping for his saddle, six-gun still in hand. The man looked fearfully towards the marshal and he fired wildly.

Bronco ducked, came up with the rifle at his shoulder, fired once, his bullet blowing Dancey clean over his prancing mount's back so that the man landed hard and twisted and somersaulted on the far side. He lay still, his smoking Colt a good four feet from his hand.

'Oh, my God, they're all dead now!' Kimble was panting, his face bearing marks of gravel and dirt, one sleeve torn. He looked accusingly at Madigan who was reloading the rifle.

The older marshal glanced up. 'Dancey's not hit bad and Brannigan's still breathing – we can still get the information we want.'

Kimble stared, open-mouthed.

'Can't you – can't you ever let a man die in peace?'

'What for? He's gonna know peace for a long, long time – if he can help me before he goes, why the hell not?'

'You can't *really* be that hard and cold, Madigan!'

Bronco smiled thinly. 'It's a hard, cold world, kid. You want to keep walking around it, you do what you have to do.'

'You mean *you* do things I've never seen anyone else do! Though I've heard of Indians just as bad.'

'Maybe that's why you're still a greenhorn instead

of a fully-fledged marshal, kid.'

'I'm not sure I want to be a fully-fledged marshal
. . . like you.'

That one actually got under Madigan's guard but
his hard, rugged face was unreadable.

'Let's go down and see if I can shock you some
more.'

CHAPTER 9

BACK TRAIL

Brannigan wasn't going to last long, though Dancey would pull through. Madigan's bullet had seared across his shoulders and the fall from the horse had knocked him senseless. He bore another wound, presumably from Brannigan's original attack, but the bullet had sliced the flesh and bounced off a rib without penetrating into the body cavity. But Dancey had lost a lot of blood, looked very white – and he was scared he was dying.

Madigan did nothing to make him think otherwise and threw Beau a warning look while the young marshal worked over the man's wound, bandaging the ribs roughly but firmly.

Madigan had hauled the shot-up gambler around to a sitting position, ignoring Brannigan's cries of pain and protest – and Kimble's disapproving looks. Deuce Brannigan, big and brutal, a typical bully and a tinhorn gambler to boot, licked involuntarily at the blood oozing from a corner of his mouth, watching Madigan closely with dulling eyes.

'You . . . gonna gimme . . . more . . . pain, Bronco?'

The marshal shrugged. 'How much you figure you can stand, Deuce?'

If possible, the gambler looked more distressed than ever. He coughed some bright blood and Madigan tore the front out of the man's fancy shirt and held the dripping red cloth before Brannigan's face.

'Coming from inside you, Deuce. You know you ain't got long, and there's things I need to know.'

'Don't – don't hurt me no more . . . Mad . . . Mad. . . .' His tongue couldn't shape the word and his jaw sagged. 'What. . . ?'

'You know what – Estrada. That twenty-five thousand bucks in the secret compartment of your cash drawer. It was meant for something special. Tell me about it, Deuce, but hurry things along, OK?'

Brannigan looked for a moment as if he might cry, startling Madigan. Breath was wheezing and rattling in his throat making sucking sounds through the wounds. One bloody hand lifted a few inches then dropped back limply into his lap. 'I . . . don't wanna die!'

'That part's outa my hands, Deuce.'

Brannigan rallied abruptly. 'Estrada's money for bribin' Gov'men' . . . men. Why he's in town . . . big trouble back in Mexico.'

'So, he's on the run and buying a way out.' It didn't really surprise Madigan, but he wanted to know the names of the men who were taking bribes.

Only unintelligible sounds came from Brannigan's scarlet mouth.

'Estrada sent money and you softened up the target. How, Deuce? Cards? A few hands dealt from the bottom of the pack, get their IOUs or names on enough markers that could wreck their careers? Big gambling losses and someone who has access to public monies don't mix too well. Makes folk suspicious . . . you keep the marker, make 'em take the bribe and you've got 'em in your pocket forever – that the deal?'

Brannigan nodded, rolling loosely.

'Where're the markers now?'

'Dunno – there was one missin', but that whore, Goldie, said she never seen . . . it. Mebbe not – Dancey or Barnes might have it. . . .'

'You were the one killed Goldie?' Madigan asked quietly, and Brannigan's eyes widened and . . . suddenly he screamed.

A blood-chilling, gargling cry wrenched from deep inside him as the pain became unbearable. Even Madigan jumped and Brannigan's body arched, thrashed briefly, then slumped, darker blood coming out of his mouth. The lawman stood slowly, aware of the pale-faced Kimble glaring at him coldly.

'You just couldn't let him die in peace, could you?'

Madigan started to deny it, but thought, *What the hell? He couldn't be bothered explaining it was just Brannigan's time to die, and he hadn't touched the man. . . .*

He walked across to where Dancey was lying, bandaged now, looking up anxiously at the older marshal whose clothes were spattered with Brannigan's blood. Bronco hunkered down.

'Brannigan thinks you might have a gambling marker that was in that cash drawer.'

Dancey stared, then shook his head quickly. 'No! I dunno nothin' about no marker. We was just after the money. Maybe Goldie. . . ?'

'Not according to Brannigan – and he was the one killed her.'

'So that's why you made him suffer!' Kimble said, standing over Madigan now.

Madigan ignored him. 'Dancey, how come you and Barnes were heading for Lexington?'

Dancey slid his gaze away quickly. 'Who said we were. . . ?' When Madigan only continued to stare he squirmed a little and shrugged. 'Barnes has a . . . gal there. Sort of.'

Kimble jumped when Madigan slapped Dancey across the face. As the young marshal stepped in, Madigan lifted a hand to stop him, without looking at him. 'Leave it, kid – Dancey's lying. He knows him and Barnes weren't busted out of the bullpen just to set 'em free – someone wanted that marker, figured they had it.' He glanced at Kimble. 'But you got to 'em first – even got 'em to help break me out. They knew they were marked for death, used you, a marshal, for protection till they were ready to run – that about how it happened, Dance?'

Rubbing his stinging face, Dancey stared apprehensively at Madigan. He licked his lips, then said in a hoarse whisper, 'There is a gal in Lexington. Barnes mailed the marker before we got throwed in the bullpen. Never told me what it was, just that we'd pick it up when we got to Lexington.'

Madigan smiled thinly. 'And you were going to make yourselves some big money by a little black-mail. You know the name on the marker, don't you?'

Dancey shook his head emphatically. 'No! Barnes handled all that! I din' even know what was in the envelope. It was just lyin' in the top cash drawer. I was more interested in seein' how much we had . . . next thing he's actin' all mysterious and tells me he mailed it away.'

'I might believe that, Dance – if you tell me his gal's name and address.'

'All I know is she lives in Lexington and—' He reared back as Madigan slapped him again. This time Kimble said nothing.

'All right! Her name's Jenny Squires. She's Barnes's sister, a widow. . . .'

'And how long d'you think it'll take Estrada to find that out!' Madigan said softly. He stood and Dancey wrenched away, grimacing, expecting a kick or a punch. 'Relax, Dance, this is your lucky day.'

'You wouldn't say that if you had my busted ribs an' a shoulder hurtin' like a bear's chewed on it.'

'Ah, got a bit of spirit again now you figure you're off the hook, eh?' Madigan turned to Kimble. 'Take Barnes's horse, Beau. We've got some hard riding to do if we're gonna get to Lexington before Estrada.'

'You think he'll—' Madigan's look made Kimble stop speaking abruptly. He nodded, embarrassed. 'Stupid question! Of course he'll kill her if he can.'

'Then let's go stop the son of a bitch!'

'Hey, what about me?' Dancey called.

Neither marshal answered and Dancey was still yelling and cussing when they rode off into the afternoon.

They crossed the Blue Ridge Mountains and headed south to Roanoke, turned west through Salem to Pearlsburg. Then skirted the southern bend of Bluestone Lake at the south tip of the Alleghenies, saving themselves a lot of tortuous mountain trails.

They replenished supplies at Princeton and learned that Estrada's private coach had passed through the town two days earlier. Using his personal letter of credit at a local bank, Kimble bought fresh horses and supplies. They cut across the bottom of West Virginia and the Big Sandy River and arrived in Kentucky just after dark.

Madigan looked up from his map. 'Estrada let Cherry think he was bound for Missouri, just making a casual stopover in Lexington. But I figure he really wants to get to that widow and recover the missing marker. If he's in a real hurry, he may not even stop at night – with a change of drivers he could snatch a little sleep in the coach while it's still rolling, get there faster.'

'What about his back-trail,' Kimble asked. 'Will he have someone to watch that?'

The marshal nodded slowly. 'Good thought, Beau. I've been charging ahead, forgetting about that. That farmer said there were three outriders, and I'm pretty sure it would be *El Halcon* riding in the coach with Estrada. Now we're drawing closer, he'll want to make sure he gets to the girl and has time to do his devil's work.'

'He'll set up an ambush for us?'

'Either that or send The Hawk on ahead to find Mrs Jenny Squires. Damn! We've lagged too far behind!'

'We could take a stage, tie the mounts on the back, and travel at night, too, while getting some rest,' Kimble suggested. 'Bound to be a stage leaving around daylight.'

Madigan nodded, pointing towards a string of lights glittering like beads, far out across the night plains.

'Best get to that town and try our luck, I guess.'

Later, when they rode in and saw lights still burning at the Wells Fargo Depot, Madigan said quietly, 'Nice work, Beau. Glad you're starting to show some interest in this deal at last. You haven't had your mind on it properly.'

Kimble smiled crookedly. 'Only on what kind of hell you're going to raise with every outlaw we catch up with, eh?'

Madigan laughed quietly. 'Yeah, on the surface that's about it. But you seem to have something deeper on your mind, kid, bitching and carping all the time. More than usual, I mean. You should've figured out a lot of that stuff for yourself – anything you want to talk about?'

'Nothing,' Kimble said shortly.

Madigan said no more. But while they were waiting for the early-morning stage to hitch up, Kimble suddenly drew a small lavender-coloured envelope from his pocket and handed it to Madigan who arched his eyebrows quizzically.

'That was delivered to me just before we set out from Washington. Go ahead – read it. I-I don't care.'

Madigan opened it slowly, unfolded the single page inside. It was brief and to the point.

On top of everything else, you've got me pregnant! What're you going to do about it?

It was signed simply with the initial E.

Madigan didn't have to ask whose name it stood for.

They had the stage to themselves on the run to the first swing-station and Madigan smoked silently, Kimble sitting stiffly beside him. After a long time, just as the swing station came in view, high up on the rise, Kimble said, 'You must be curious about that note!'

Madigan shrugged. 'I already know it's from Emmaline Cattrell and that you must be kinda churned-up inside, remembering the Virginia society gal you put in the family way before your pa pulled a few strings and got you into the Marshals' Service as a way out.'

Kimble flushed and looked down at the gritty floorboards between his dusty boots. 'Ye-es. There is a similarity. And they say lightning never strikes twice in the same place!'

'Well, it wasn't the same place, exactly, was it?'

Beau smiled ruefully. 'I guess not. I'm not really a

philanderer, Bronco, despite what it seems. I-I was genuinely fond of both those young ladies – still am, otherwise I would not have. . . . Well, perhaps it wasn't love in the sense of the romantic stories, but there was genuine affection, at least, on my side.'

'Now it's time to pay the piper. Decided what you're going to do?'

Kimble sighed. 'I know my father won't help this time and – well, I guess Parminter wouldn't be pleased. And Senator Cattrell doesn't seem very approachable.'

'First you've gotta approach Emmaline, I'd think. See what she wants you to do about it.'

'Oh, she'll want to marry me, that's pretty much for sure, but I'm not ready for marriage. . . .'

His words trailed off as he saw Madigan's hard-set face. 'Everyone makes mistakes, kid, but be man enough to do the right thing to correct 'em.'

Kimble flushed. After a pause he said, 'I know what the right thing to do is, Bronco, but I just don't want to do it, to be honest! Oh, I'm not saying that Emmaline isn't nice-looking and charming, but . . . well, I don't think I want to be part of the Cattrell family.'

'This is something you have to work out for yourself, Beau, you and the girl. You already said you know what you should do.'

'And you think I should go ahead and do it?' Kimble asked but Madigan refused to answer. Beau shook his head. 'All the married marshals I know have desk jobs. I don't want that.' He looked hard at Madigan. 'Anyway, how come you never married?'

'Leave it alone, kid,' Madigan replied curtly.

'Well, despite what I said a little time back, I guess I wouldn't mind being like you, Bronco. I mean, tough but fair – by your own lights – fast with a gun, mean when you have to be. Someone other men, even outside the service, look up to, but could you still be that way if you'd gotten married?'

Madigan rolled a cigarette and, as he reached for a match said, 'We'll never know, will we? And it's nothing to do with this, anyway. Hey! Here's the swing-station. Four passengers waiting . . . a woman and three men.'

Kimble took the hint and fell silent as the stage rolled into the way-station yard and a couple of roustabouts in frayed overalls came running to grab the lead horses and give them nosebags and water.

When he saw Madigan looking levelly at him, Kimble eased back in his seat, tipped his hat over his face, obviously going to take the opportunity to snatch a few winks of sleep. Or he wanted to give that impression. . . .

Bronco Madigan turned his attention to the men who were getting ready to board, one hanging back, holding the arm of the woman who seemed a little frail and unsteady on her feet.

The others were not gentlemen, not waiting to allow the man to help the woman into the coach before them. They seemed eager to see who the passengers were already sitting inside. It took Madigan about three seconds to figure both of them were hired gunfighters.

They had to be waiting for him and Kimble.

CHAPTER 10

HARD RIDING

With his right hand, Madigan reached behind him and turned down the handle on the inner face of the door, unlocking it. He thrust his shoulder and body weight against the door and with his left hand fisted-up the startled Kimble's vest front and then heaved backwards.

The door crashed open and Madigan began to fall, dragging Kimble with him. The young marshal was yelling, but then Madigan freed his vest and Beau had to look after himself, hands thrust out to break his fall.

Before he touched the ground, guns roared and he happened to be twisting on to his shoulders to take the jolt of the impact and saw bullets ripping through the flimsy plywood of the stage-coach. Splinters flailed the air and he threw an arm across his face to protect his eyes.

By then Madigan was rolling away from the coach

in a cloud of dust, spinning on to his back and thrusting up, six-gun blazing. He shot through the coach, between the seats and swinging door, at the two gunmen crouched on the far side. One man, leaning against the coach side grunted and was slammed away from the vehicle, falling to one knee. There was blood on his back where a bullet had seared across and he staggered up as his companion, a medium-sized *hombre* in neat grey clothes, reached under his frock coat and brought out a sawn-off shotgun.

He wrenched the splintered door all the way open and blasted the first barrel through the interior of the cabin. Leather shredded, kapok padding and stuffing swirled and filled the air like a snow storm. Both Kimble and Madigan staggered back, coughing.

The man in grey jumped into the shattered cabin of the rocking coach as the roustabouts, fearful but loyal to their boss, fought to hold the terrified team from breaking away. The man swung down the sawn-off in Madigan's direction and the marshal threw himself sideways just as Kimble fired.

Beau's bullet rocked the man in the coach so that he tumbled on to the shot-torn seat. Then Madigan slammed two shots into him and skidded in the gravel as he ran around the rear of the vehicle, hurriedly reloading. Kimble climbed over the bloody, sliding body and triggered at a running figure making for the station buildings. The man in grey fell against his legs spoiling his aim, and the running man turned in mid-stride, swung up his gun as Kimble floundered.

Madigan came around the rear of the bullet-riddled coach and his Colt roared. The shot took the man high in the chest and flung him violently into the side of the building. Then the station manager appeared on the veranda with a Savage shotgun and cut loose with both barrels.

The gunman slid down, leaving a wide smear of blood and traces of blown-out internal organs on the logs. He sat down and his head drooped as if he was asleep. He was, but it was one from which he would never awake. . . .

Coughing in the kapok cloud and dust and billowing gunsmoke, Kimble and Madigan made their way to the station's main building. The man with the frail-looking woman was huddled over her just under the railing of the porch. Madigan knelt beside him.

'Your wife all right, mister?'

Even as he asked, he saw the woman was alive, pale and shaken, her clothes dirt-smeared, but she was alive and that was enough. The man helped her up, then turned on Madigan, his face enraged. But he stopped when the marshal lifted a hand.

'I know it's hard to take, feller, but you and your missus are both OK – settle for that, all right?'

The woman placed a hand on her husband's forearm and gave Madigan a nod and a nervous smile. 'It's all right, Artie – really,' she whispered.

Artie was still mad but there was something about Madigan which made him swallow his angry words. 'Seems a man ain't safe anywhere, these days!'

'Sorry it happened, friend,' Kimble said coming up and smiling warmly at the woman. He glanced at the station agent. 'How about some coffee, or maybe something a little stronger for the lady?'

'Bring her inside,' the man said, then looked at Madigan. 'I wanta few words with you.'

'Likewise.' Madigan fully loaded his gun again before holstering it, smiling faintly as Kimble played the gentleman and took one of the woman's arms, on the opposite side to that of her husband. They went inside and Madigan rolled a cigarette under the wide-eyed stares of the roustabouts as they unhitched the still terrified team and turned them loose in the corrals.

The agent's name was Miller and he knew Madigan of old. Later, in the barn, sharing a stone jug of illegal moonshine, the big, fat man said, wiping a pudgy wrist across his mouth, 'Din' I read somewheres where you was on the dodge, Bronco? I mean, it didn't make sense but. . . .'

'It makes sense, Hondo,' Madigan told him. 'But you don't need to know the details.'

Miller held up one hand, offering the jug to Kimble who was just arriving. He refused politely. The agent glanced at Madigan. 'Beau can't drink much.'

There was enough in Madigan's choice of words to tell Miller that Kimble either had or was trying to get over a drinking problem – which he was – and so far making a pretty good job of it.

'Uh-huh. Knew when them sonuvers was left behind by that Mex there was gonna be trouble for someone.'

'Who else was with the Mex, besides these two, Hondo?'

' 'Nother white man and a tough-lookin' Mex with a beak on him like a starvin' buzzard.'

'*El Halcon?*' asked Kimble quietly, and Madigan nodded.

'Hear anything they said – about where they were going; when, any names mentioned?'

Miller shook his head, took another swig from the jug. 'They din' talk much. They called the older Mex Señor Estrada. He was polite enough, in a cold way, thanked me for the meal and so on, paid in advance for the room for them two rats you just killed.'

Madigan looked disappointed that there wasn't more, and then Miller, wiping his mouth again, said, 'Other thing I heard was somethin' about a gal. Dunno where, nor her name, but from what they said, seems she's in a heap of trouble with that Mex. I sure wouldn't like to be her, anyways.'

'What exactly did they say, sir?' Kimble asked, and Miller raised his eyebrows, flicked his gaze to Madigan.

'He ain't your regular kinda sidekick, Bronco.'

'No. He's got manners, been taught to respect his elders – but he asked a good question, Hondo.'

Miller grunted, thinking. 'Estrada said somethin' like, "After we're through with her, she's all yours," and that hook-nosed son of a bitch said, "And after I'm through with her no one'll have any use for her!" '

Hondo Miller produced a couple of well-muscled, long-pacing mounts for them and they transferred their warbags and grubsacks and rifle scabbards after saddling and left in a cloud of dust. Hondo's Indian woman gave them some hunks of cold roast beef and a couple of cold but fresh biscuits to munch on as they rode.

The horses lived up to Hondo's build-up and claims about speed and stamina. The riders were ready to fall asleep in the saddles, but the mounts showed no signs of tiring, kept up the punishing, gruelling pace across the Cumberland Plateau. Madigan figured to let the horses run until *they* decided they wanted to rest.

He figured it would be too late to help Jenny Squires now, but at least they could stay on Estrada's trail and square whatever they had to when they caught him up.

Then next morning, early, for they had started out of their camp by a creek and small waterfall before the sun rose, they reined down on a rise, walked the mounts behind some trees and used Kimble's Zeiss field-glasses to get a closer look at the dark blob way out on the plains.

'By Godfrey, it's a black, leather-top coach!' exclaimed Kimble, playing with the focusing wheel carefully. 'Ye-es – doors are open and I can see two men sitting inside, one's smoking.'

'Where's the driver and the other white man Hondo said was with Estrada?'

Madigan was reaching impatiently for the Zeiss glasses as he spoke, jostled Kimble deliberately. 'Lemme take a look, Beau.'

Madigan already had the glasses in his hand and Kimble tightened his lips, shook his head slowly as the older marshal adjusted focus. 'Hell, you must have queer eyesight, kid, this'll take me five minutes to get it adjusted.'

Kimble smiled thinly: he couldn't let that chance go by. 'They say a man's sight alters a lot as he gets older, Bronco – starts to deteriorate. Like the rest of him.'

Madigan swivellled his gaze past the eye-piece briefly and grunted, but Kimble's smile widened at his small victory. Then Bronco said, 'That's the two Mexes in the coach, all right – be Estrada and The Hawk. No sign of the driver but I think the white man Hondo mentioned is over under those trees. Might even have his field-glasses trained on us.'

Kimble instinctively hunkered down and moved a couple of paces deeper into the trees' shadow. Madigan's lips twitched slightly as he moved the glasses slowly. 'Yeah, I think I see a faint haze of tobacco smoke coming out of those trees ... So there's two in the coach, one in the brush. Why?'

Kimble hesitated. 'Well, there's got to be something wrong for it to be abandoned out there. All four wheels look OK except maybe that off-front one is slanted more than normal. One of the horses is favouring a left forefoot but I don't think it's anything serious. Maybe just resting it more comfortably bent up that way. . . .'

'I see all that, but where's the damn driver?'

'One of the team horses is missing. Maybe the driver took it and rode on ahead to get help in the next town. . . .'

'Which would have to be Stanton, or maybe Clay

118

City,' cut in Madigan, who was still using the Zeiss.

'It's the front axle!' Kimble said suddenly, pointing. 'You can hardly make it out underneath but it looks as if its sagging. It's been broken and they've made an attempt to repair it. Looks like it wasn't successful.'

Madigan scowled: Kimble had seen all that *without* the aid of the glasses! 'Yeah, likely busted it down at that ford we crossed. The tracks were all messed-up but I'd guess they hit the ford too fast and struck an underwater rock. Lashed a sapling across but it's given out again. Driver should've cut a spare while he was at it – I'll bet Estrada ain't happy about the delay!'

'Be a lot less happy when we ride in on him.'

Madigan handed Kimble back the excellent field-glasses. 'Must get me a pair of them some time. No, Beau. We ain't riding in on that trio.'

Kimble frowned. 'But we can take them, Bronco! We're both good rifle shots and—'

'And at the moment they're stuck out here and Jenny Squires should still be alive in Lexington – we'll go and make sure she stays that way.'

'Well, capturing Estrada will do that.'

'Mebbe – but *El Halcon*'s no one to mess with and I dunno who that other white man is. Fact that he's holed-up in the trees while his boss sits in the coach shows he takes his job seriously. And there's a heap of open ground for us to cross before we get within shooting range.'

Kimble nodded. 'I guess you're right. But we'll have to do some hard riding, take a long detour around and cut through the pass in that line of hills, otherwise they'll see us. The driver could get back and have that axle repaired before we reach Lexington – and they'll just have a straight run in, get there ahead of us.'

Madigan admitted that was a possibility. But he hadn't liked the way Hondo had imitated *El Halcon* and what he had said about the girl being of no use to anyone after he was through with her. . . .

Madigan had seen too many women over the years who had died in utter terror as a result of some sadistic, lecherous bastard living out his perverted fantasies with them. One of those women could have been his wife if she had lived. . . . If he could prevent some other woman from that kind of fate, he would – no matter what it took.

'We ride flat out and we'll hit that pass before noon, then cross the flats, skirt Stanton and Clay City, and take the trail straight into Lexington. That's when the real work begins. Finding the woman, getting her away safely before Estrada has a chance to turn his killers loose.'

Kimble moved quickly towards his mount, face grim. 'If he hasn't already sent someone on ahead.'

'Then what are we standing around talking for?'

They saw Stanton in the distance even before they left the high pass and started down to the plains. It was a scattering of buildings, with straggling lines of houses meandering off at almost every point of the compass. There wasn't much paint showing in the town and the overall impression was one of drabness.

But there were two riders racing out along the winding trail back to the hills where they had last seen Estrada's stranded coach. A third horse, carrying obviously heavily loaded panniers, trailed behind one of the riders.

'Leader could be the stagecoach driver,' Kimble opined, reaching for his Zeiss glasses but changing his mind. 'Picked himself up a workman and a new axle by the looks of that long pole poking out of one of the panniers.'

Madigan didn't see anything to comment about: what Kimble said was obvious enough. But he narrowed his gaze slightly. He knew the signs in his sidekick when the man was worried or on edge. And Beau was exhibiting some of them now: a restlessness in the saddle, looking around constantly, lips pulled back over his very white teeth as if he was trying to make a hard decision.

'Want to say your piece?'

Kimble snapped his head around, smiled thinly. 'Your eyesight's OK close up, Bronco! Well, I was just thinking. Skirting Stanton is going to take a lot of riding, but if we went straight through – see Main? It's like a carpenter's straightedge, cuts the town almost in half. Reckon we'd save an hour by riding through there. No one'll take any notice of us, a couple of riders in a hurry passing through.'

Madigan studied the town, then swung his eyes to Kimble. 'You could be right, but first, you tell me what you want to do in town.'

Kimble tried to look innocent but it took a lot more acting than he had in him to fool a man like

Bronco Madigan. Finally, he nodded, tightening his lips. 'OK – I've been looking at the telegraph line as we rode through the pass. Goes straight into Stanton.'

'You want to send a wire? Dunno as I'll allow that.'

The young marshal didn't like it but he swallowed his anger and said, 'It'll only take a couple of minutes – it's a very short message – OK?'

'Kid, it's who you're sending the wire to that interests me. We're on assignment and s'posed to stay away from telegraph depots except in a real emergency. And it's best if no one recognizes me as a fugitive.'

'This has nothing to do with the assignment, Bronco, I swear.' Kimble was sitting rigidly in the saddle now and held Madigan's steady gaze.

Madigan nodded. 'I reckon I can take you at your word, Beau.'

That brought a grin to Kimble's anxious face: it meant a lot to him to have Madigan trust him this way.

'Thanks, Bronco! I'll be quick, meet you at the bridge over the creek far end of town.'

And he was as good as his word, was actually at the hump-backed wooden bridge several minutes before Madigan.

They didn't speak, simply cleared the drab town and lifted their mounts along the trail to Clay City.

After that, there would be just thirty miles more of hard riding and they would come to the outskirts of Lexington – and soon after learn if Jenny Squires was still alive and had the gambler's marker they needed so desperately.

CHAPTER 11

DECOY

It was an easy chore locating Jenny Squires in Lexington – or just on the outskirts.

Kimble simply walked into the local law office, flashed his badge and some paper identification and told the sheriff he wanted some information.

'Always glad to co-operate with the Marshals' Service. What d'you want to know?'

The sheriff was a fit-looking man about forty-five or six, balding, with a deep voice and a no-nonsense look to his somewhat battered face. He had two more deputies working at small desks that were cluttered with paperwork. Kimble figured a man who liked plenty of records and information on hand was just the kind of man he needed right now.

'Looking for a widow named Jenny Squires. All I know is she lives in Lexington.'

Sheriff Doucette eased back in his chair and there was a slight tightening of his features.

'Widow Squires don't actually live in Lexington,' he said slowly. 'More on the northern outskirts, the Fayette side of town.'

Kimble wasn't conversant with Lexington but he caught a tone in the sheriff's voice that said either the erstwhile widow or the location of her address was not to his liking. 'That's OK – I can find my way there. Got a street address?'

Doucette shook his head. ' 'Fraid not. The good widow runs herself a market garden out there, small-holding, but she puts a lot of energy into it – maybe too much at times.'

The marshal couldn't resist asking what the sheriff meant.

'Well, she cuts her prices to the bone. Only works a few field hands and pays 'em in kind. Might not sound such a good idea but it is for the field hands – they all live in town, with families, and they live pretty damn good with Jenny Squires' produce. What little money they make they can spend on – well, whatever they like, I guess.'

He paused and Kimble nodded slowly. 'I guess this doesn't go down so well with other market gardeners who pay their field hands in cash and have other overheads.'

Doucette looked mildly surprised that Kimble had picked that up right off but nodded. 'Yeah – been a little trouble now and again.' He allowed himself a half-smile. 'Bunch of tough guys near wet their pants when they run up agin Widow Squires in a protective mood – she shot a couple, completely unrepentant, and the town's behind her, including the judge, so

124

she never even got a fine.' He shook his head slowly. 'I leave her alone mostly, so if you want her for breaking the law or somesuch, you take heed and go easy on the approach in case she shoots your head off . . .'

Kimble smiled. 'No, nothing like that. Thanks, Sheriff. I'll remember your co-operation.'

'Sounds feisty,' Madigan commented when Kimble came back to their camp-site and told him what he had found out. 'We might's well ride out there – plenty of time before sundown.'

Kimble nodded and Madigan paused, seeing the sober look on the young marshal's face and a kind of far-away glint to his eyes.

'You all right?'

Beau stirred, frowned and said pretty darn curtly, 'Of course I am – just – tired, that's all. We've done a lot of riding, Bronco. I guess it's beginning to tell.'

Madigan grunted, then suddenly reached out and lifted a folded yellow form from the man's shirt pocket. Kimble grabbed but missed and his eyes were narrowed as he held out his hand. 'Give me that back!'

Madigan made no attempt to open the folded paper but he waved it in front of Kimble's face. 'Telegraph form – got an answer already to the wire you sent in Stanton?'

'Yes.' Kimble snatched the paper. 'It's private.'

'Sure, but seems to me whatever it says is not good news.'

'You never mind what it says!'

Madigan shrugged and checked his rifle and six-gun before mounting. Kimble still stood beside his horse, suddenly walked across and looked up at Madigan.

He held up the telegraph form. 'You can read it.'

'I don't need to, kid – like you said, it's private.'

Kimble insisted and Madigan shrugged, opened the form, saw that it was addressed to Kimble 'care of General Delivery, Lexington, Kentucky' – which told him Kimble had planned on picking up the reply there all along. The message was brief, unsigned.

No!

Madigan looked down slowly. 'Emphatic.'

'That wire from Stanton was to ask Emmaline to marry me. What you're holding is her reply.'

Bronco pursed his lips slowly, folded the paper and handed it back. 'Well, you offered and it was the right thing to do. Of course, there are other . . . alternatives . . . which ain't quite so right, but—'

'I'll have to see her when we get back to Washington.' Kimble shook his head briefly. 'I thought marriage was what she wanted. I'm not saying I'm disappointed she refused, but – well, I-I – dunno.'

'Like you said, see her when you get back – which may not be for quite some time. This marker could lead us almost anywhere, even down to Mexico. You handle that, Beau? It could be months and you'll have this on your mind. If you want to be relieved, I can handle it for you and you could go back and settle things. Parminter'll send someone else; Clete

Hannigan has tangled with Estrada before. . . .'

Kimble was flushed now. 'No, I don't want to be relieved! I'm a marshal on assignment and I'll see it through. I won't allow my private concerns to inter-fere. And I'm kind of disappointed that you even mentioned it, Bronco.'

'So am I, Beau, but you made the right answer. Can't do any more from here, so let's go talk to this Jenny Squires.'

Which turned out to be a little harder than expected.

Her market garden covered a couple of acres and there were three sunken wells for water that Madigan could see, wooden channels running from each well to a series of neat gardens. There was a whip-style bucket-lifter which swivelled so as to allow the buck-ets of water to be tipped into the channels with ease.

'Knows what she's about,' allowed Madigan, as he and Kimble rode down the narrow dirt paths between rows of healthy-looking vegetables.

Hard on his last word came the crack of a rifle and his hat spun off his head, and would have sailed away except for the tie-thong catching under his jaw. The thin leather seared his flesh and he cussed even as he threw himself out of the saddle, snatching his rifle from the scabbard.

Kimble's horse pranced and its forefeet trampled some lettuce. This time the rifle cracked twice and the young marshal yelled as a bullet whipped air past his face and another ricocheted from the saddle-horn. He took off his hat, crouching low over his horse now, steadying it on to the dirt path.

127

He waved his hat in a wide arc, calling, 'Take it easy! Federal Marshals here!'

'Great work, Beau!' gritted Madigan, crouched by the rock wall of one of the wells, rifle in hand. 'If that's Estrada's man in that log cabin, he knows he's got the right targets now!'

'It's the woman!' Kimble said confidently. 'I saw her as she moved across the window!' He raised his voice. 'Ma'am! We mean you no harm!'

'Will you shut up! You saw her but that doesn't mean she wasn't pushed across so you could see her and make a better target of yourself – just like you're doing!'

Then the door in the cabin opened and a smallish woman with grey-streaked black hair stood there in mud spattered canvas trousers and boots, and an untidy man's shirt that was too big for her. She also held a long-barrelled Henry rifle.

'I can see your badge glinting, Marshal!' an Irish-sounding voice called. 'I'm good enough to shoot the middle right out of it – so you and your friend move mighty easy and show me empty hands or I start shootin' in earnest!'

They obeyed, walked their mounts forward slowly, hands raised. She made them dismount in the front yard covering them with the Henry while she examined Kimble's badge and papers. She had a handsome enough face except it was hard around the mouth and her eyes were wary.

Madigan spoke before she said anything, 'It's about your brother – Andy Barnes.'

She stiffened and white-knuckled the rifle and said

in a surpisingly quiet and controlled voice, 'I don't believe I have a brother.'

Kimble looked uncertainly at Madigan who spoke quietly. 'I'm sorry to tell you, ma'am, that he's dead.'

They watched her get herself under control and she spoke in the same calm tone. 'If that is all you wanted with me, then I thank you, gentlemen, but I have to say in all honesty, it doesn't matter a fig to me. He was not a decent man, Andrew Barnes. He robbed our parents, killed two of our kin, caused my husband's untimely death.'

Madigan cut in. 'All we want to know is did he send you an envelope with a paper he wanted you to keep for him?'

Her eyes narrowed. 'So! That's what this is about!'

'Did he send you such a paper, ma'am?' Beau asked.

'Yes – I got a letter, didn't recognize the handwriting. He wanted me to keep the "special" paper as he called it and he would come collect some time – and then we would all be rich!' She snorted. 'That was all Andrew ever thought of! Money! Getting rich – no matter how, and certainly not honestly.'

'You still got the paper, Mrs Squires?' cut in Madigan.

Her eyes flicked to him, looked him over. 'You're a hard one, I can tell it wouldn't surprise me if you were the one killed Andrew.'

'He was ambushed by a tinhorn gambler, missus . . . have you still got that paper?'

'Well, that seems a fitting end for Andrew Barnes. . . .' Try as she might, she could not *quite* keep the catch from her voice. 'No, I burnt the paper. I wanted no part of it. I knew it must be tainted.'

Madigan smothered a curse and Kimble said, 'Did you happen to look at the paper first, ma'am?'

'Oh, yes, It was a gambling IOU.'

'Who signed it?' Madigan asked softly. 'Whose name was on the paper?'

She took her time answering, looking from one to the other. 'It was hard to make out, little more than a scrawl, but I think the name was "Cottrell" or something similar.'

The marshals were preparing to leave when Jenny Squires offered them some cool lemonade, or coffee if they preferred. They decided to settle for the lemonade and Madigan could see now that she was considerably sobered by the news about her brother. She might have said she detested Andy Barnes and seemed to have good reason for disliking him – if not actually hating the man – but underneath the feisty, independent exterior she was a warm and compassionate human being. Losing a brother in a world where you and he are the only remaining carriers of the family blood-line would get to most people deep down where they lived.

The lemonade was good and Kimble was feeling sorry for the lone woman. Maybe Madigan was, too, but you would never know it by his expression. Beau cleared his throat.

'You're sure about the signature on that IOU, ma'am?' he asked. 'It definitely was "Cottrell"?'

Madigan watched him levelly even as he sipped his second glass of lemonade. They were sitting just inside the open kitchen door, catching the breeze.

'That's what it looked like but I didn't bother to study it – I allowed my temper to get the better of me and threw it in the fire.' She stopped abruptly, looking past the shoulders of the marshals who were sitting opposite her, side-on to the door. 'Seems it's my day for visitors!'

Madigan rounded so fast he almost toppled the straightback chair as his right hand instinctively fell to his six-gun butt.

Estrada's leather-topped black coach was rocking into the market garden, with one outrider who was unsheathing his rifle from the saddle scabbard.

'What on earth do they think they're doing!' Jenny Squires jumped to her feet and moved past the lawman swiftly, snatching up her Henry from where she had leaned it against the wall by the door. She raised her voice as she lunged outside before Madigan could stop her. '*Get out of there! Get off my gardens, you damn fools!*'

The coach was deliberately cutting across the rows of neat gardens now, hoofs and wheels destroying the ready-for-picking vegetables. The outrider seemed to be staying on the narrow tracks but the driver of the coach was whipping up the team and the vehicle was wreaking havoc with the gardens. She started shooting as Madigan came out of the house, grabbed her and flung her unceremoniously back into the kitchen. He dived after her as guns cracked from the approaching coach. Kimble kicked the door shut and dropped the bar across, as bullets thudded into the woodwork.

Dishevelled, angry, Jenny Squires had a few un-ladylike remarks to make, shook her arm free as Kimble helped her to her feet. She snatched up her rifle. Madigan was standing beside the window, but the shutter was only half-raised, and he had to crouch in order to get a shot at the coach.

Splinters flew, but he fired and his lead kicked the driver over the side, flailing. The team, reins loose now, swerved and the coach swayed drunkenly. Madigan could see the new wood of the front axle, deliberately shot the offside leader of the team. The horse dropped quickly and the others reared and swerved and whinnied as they piled-up on the carcass. In seconds, the narrow black coach teetered, then fell on to its side, being dragged a few feet before it reared up and came crashing down on its roof. Wood supports splintered and poked through torn leather. The wheels spun dizzyingly as the dust settled.

Then the Henry whipped to Jenny's shoulder as the wounded driver lurched upright, staggering, clasping a bloody arm. She fired and the man went down abruptly. 'That'll teach you to drive your lousy coach through my vegetables!'

She lunged for the door and Madigan snapped, 'Beau!'

Kimble was already heading her off. 'Easy, ma'am. Those men came to kill you and we haven't accounted for all of them yet!'

His words stopped her, made her blink. 'Kill me?'

'They think you still have that IOU.'

'But I haven't – I told you, I—'

'If they know you've even seen it they'll kill you anyway.'

'Wh-who are they?' Truly concerned now.

'Men your brother stole from,' Madigan told her flatly. 'Then he passed on that IOU to you, knowing they'd come after you and kill you if they got wind of it.'

His words certainly shook Jenny which was what Maidgan intended. As she absorbed them, he swung up his rifle, seeing two men in Mexican garb crawling out of the overturned coach.

'Watch that other one!' Bronco snapped to Kimble, as he triggered and saw dirt kick into the face of the man he knew as Estrada. The Mexican reared back, clawing at his eyes and the other, the one with the large beak of a nose, *El Halcon*, came up to his knees, left hand chopping at the hammer of a six-gun braced against his hip. The bullets walked across the window shutter, slivers of wood thrumming close to Madigan's face as he ducked.

Kimble's Mannlicher cracked in two fast shots, the bolt sliding sibilantly in the dim kitchen. The white man, dismounted now, ran in a crouch for the wall of one of the wells. Kimble triggered again and the man catapulted forward, tumbling head over heels, his rifle flying from his grip as his head crashed hard against the stonework. He fell on to his back and lay still.

Madigan noted all this and slammed away the prop holding the window shutter. It crashed against the frame, ragged holes allowing sunlight to stream in. The marshal was already moving, gesturing at Kimble.

'Rattle the bar like it's stuck and won't open, then duck!'

He pushed Jenny down, who was starting to her feet, and she sat down hard with a *whoosh!* of air as he ran through the short passage to the front of the house. He heard the bar on the kitchen door rattling, then The Hawk's six-gun fired again and by that time, Madigan was out the front door and leaping over the porch rail. Crouching, he ran back down the side of the house, paused at the rear corner, then stepped out and fired his rifle from the hip. The Hawk staggered and rolled, hurriedly crawled behind the upturned coach.

As Bronco ran forward, Kimble came out through the kitchen door, long rifle held at the ready across his chest. Then Madigan skidded to a stop, not believing his eyes: *El Halcon*, the supposedly devoted bodyguard of Estrada, ran to where the white gunfighter's horse was, leapt into the saddle and spurred away, guthooks ripping at the animal's flesh. It was such a surprise to Madigan that The Hawk was gone before he could lift the rifle and take a shot. Kimble fired but it was wild – and far too late.

'What happened?' the young marshal asked, as he panted up beside him.

Bronco shook his head. 'I'm not sure – something's wrong here. *El Halcon* would never run out on Estrada.' As he spoke, he saw that the white gunfighter was starting to come around, obviously not badly injured. 'Watch him, Beau.'

Then Madigan went to where Estrada lay sprawled on his face. The man was still breathing and Madigan set down his rifle, drew his Colt, cocked it and placed the barrel against the Mexican's head as he turned him over.

His breath hissed as he sat back on his hams. No wonder *El Halcon* had run to save his own skin.

This wounded, rotund Mexican at Madigan's feet wasn't Felipe Estrada.

He was a decoy.

And Madigan had fallen for it.

CHAPTER 12

DEVIL'S WORK

While Kimble kept an eye on the dazed and bloody gunfighter who had ripped a quarter-size hole in his head when he fell against the well's rock wall, Madigan gave his attention to the man who was masquerading as Estrada.

He was wounded under the left arm but not badly, and although he had the appearance of an expanded balloon, he cut something of a comic figure. But there was cold determination in his eyes. Madigan roughly bandaged his wound, ignoring the man's Spanish expletives. He figured the man was tougher than he looked.

'Relax, *amigo*, this is nothing – I'm just getting you in a fit condition to stand up to my questioning.'

The hard eyes widened and something went out of them. He shuttled his gaze across to Kimble who had disarmed the white man and was attending to his wound, washing the blood and dirt from his features.

'You had best not play with me, *señor*. You must know who I am.'

'Matter of fact I don't – you look a lot like Estrada but you ain't him.'

There was sweat on the round face with its jet-black moustache and sideburns, giving the man a greasy appearance. 'I am Don Felipe y Ignacio Estrada – you have heard of me. You know I have the power of *El Presidente* behind me. You will do well to remember these things, I think, my friend.'

'Now, that's one thing I ain't, mister – not your friend, but I am your enemy and could be your executioner unless you come to your senses and quit this act.' Abruptly, Madigan backhanded the impostor hard across the face. He cried out in pain and blood trickled from a corner of his mouth.

'Not again, Bronco!' Kimble said. 'Can't you interrogate anybody without—'

'Set those damn horses free, Beau,' Madigan gritted, pointing to the struggling coach team, 'and watch that gunfighter closely.'

The young marshal obeyed, tight-lipped, and Bronco slapped his prisoner again. The man's head crunched against the iron tyre of the coach wheel he rested against. His eyes almost crossed. Then Madigan grabbed the dazed Mexican's right hand, stood up and placed his boot across the wrist, pinning it to the ground. His Colt slid out of leather and the cocking of the hammer brought clarity and rising fear to the dark eyes as the barrel was pressed against the base of his thumb.

'That there digit is what gives us so-called human

beings one big advantage over most of the animal world, *amigo*, they call it a prehensile thumb and if you didn't have it – well, you'd have one helluva time trying to pick up things or holding them. You don't believe me, just curl it in towards your palm and use your fingers only to loosen your belt, or unknot your neckerchief. Go on. Try it.'

The man's sweat soaked his dust-spattered clothes in dark patches, dripped from his jowls and even the ends of his moustache. He swallowed. His voice was that of a child.

'Please, *señor*! I beg you! I-I am only an actor! This is a-a role I play! I mean no real harm! Señor Estrada, he tell me, "You play it hard and mean, *amigo*, be arrogant, be loud, but make sure your passing is noticed and remembered. Make sure it is Felipe Estrada who is remembered as having passed this way or that way. You do this and I pay you well. You fail me and *El Halcon* will pay you in another way, *comprende*?" This, I swear, is all I can tell you, *señor*!'

Madigan almost believed him. Studying the man more closely now he grabbed one side of the drooping moustache and yanked suddenly. The man gasped and reared back as the hair came free of the spirit-based adhesive. One end of the closest bushy sideburn lifted and brought more gasps from the Mexican, but Madigan didn't bother ripping it right off.

He had seen enough.

So, he pressed the muzzle of the Colt harder into the base of the man's thumb. 'Where were you to go and exactly what were you to do? *Exactly* – and don't

138

give me that hogwash about being an innocent actor in all of this or . . .'

He ground the gun muzzle hard into the thumb and the Mexican writhed and groaned. 'No! No!' He was breathing heavily and gasping and wheezing in his fear. 'I am Renaldo – Don Felipe's stand-in. I take his place when he needs me to—'

'OK, Renaldo – but first, let's not have any more about *Don* Felipe. Estrada's no don, he's a toad. Next, if he keeps you on call, you do a lot more than strut about with that false hair on your face pretending to be Estrada. You have a mean look, Renaldo, and I'm damn sure Estrada would exploit that meanness.'

'No, no – it is a calculated thing, *señor* – I make myself look mean. As I said, I am an actor. I have the discipline and . . . I show you!' He writhed about, face contorting and . . . suddenly the Colt exploded.

Renaldo leapt a foot in the air, screaming as he clutched his bloody hand against his chest, drooling and crying in pain. Kimble stared at the bloody stump and the mangled thumb that had been blown almost into his lap. The white gunman stared hard, too, and while his expression didn't change, his swallowing was audible.

'What the *hell*, Bronco?' Kimble demanded. 'That wasn't necessary!'

It had been accidental. Felipe's abrupt writhing, sweat on Madigan's hand, and the hammer had slipped. But Madigan saw no need to explain this – to Kimble or anyone. He tossed Renaldo his own neckerchief and watched the man awkwardly wad it over the bloody stump where his thumb had been. 'You ready to tell me what I want to know now, Renaldo? Because if you ain't, you've still got another thumb – and lots more interesting body parts.'

Renaldo's contorted face writhed as he tried to agree through his moans and groans. Madigan didn't even glance at Kimble, whose face tightened. But then Renaldo began to talk. And, all the time, the white gunfighter lay there with his head bandaged, watching and listening in silence.

Renaldo sobbed and cursed his way through his story, interspersed with spasms of pain from his shattered hand. It was still bleeding but Madigan made no move to dress the wound, despite the Mexican's pleas, and he waved Kimble back when the young marshal started forward.

'Better this way.'

Kimble's mouth tightened. 'Who for? You?'

'Well, who the hell you think I meant? Now just watch that gunman, Beau, he looks like he might try something.'

The gunfighter had half his face sheathed in bandages down one side, nearest Madigan. The eye just showing, glinted, but he turned away and sagged against the wall, obviously feeling plenty of pain still. Renaldo was desperately afraid he was going to lose his other thumb – or other personal body parts – and he did not hold back. Madigan was waiting for the gunman to jump in on some of the things Renaldo revealed, but he didn't and the marshal figured that maybe, after all, he was no more than hired help, not usually kept on Estrada's payroll. He would remember that when he came to question him. . . .

Meantime, Renaldo revealed that he had 'often' impersonated Estrada, allowing the man to apparently be in two places at once. In some cases, it gave Estrada the perfect alibi when he decided to personally kill some enemy or rape the wife or sister or sweetheart of someone he was pressuring to give him what he wanted.

Madigan wondered how long it would be before Estrada figured that using Renaldo in this way he had put tremendous power into the hands of the fat little actor – when he did, of course, Renaldo would be a dead man. . . .

'OK, you've filled in enough background,' the marshal told the grey-faced Mexican. He gave him a drink of water. 'Get on with your present chore – why are you impersonating Estrada down here? Where is he? Still in Washington. . . ?'

Madigan was surprised to see the beginnings of a smile twitch the Mexican's purplish, bitten lips, and he knew he had underestimated Renaldo. This was the thing Madigan wanted to know – not his previous association with Estrada. So this was the tool that Renaldo, in all his pain and terror, could hold over the lawman. Make him do what he wished before he told him what he wanted to know.

He might be frightened out of his skin by what could happen to him, but he was working up the resolve that would allow him to, figuratively, hold a gun to Madigan's head until he obtained what he wanted.

'It is imperative, *señor*, that Felipe Estrada is known to be here in Kentucky at this time,' Renaldo said slowly, his breath catching as he tried to ignore the pain that refused to be ignored. Tears ran down his face but he would not look away from Madigan's hard glare. 'He must be seen.'

'Keep going, Renaldo, you're doing fine. Why is it necessary that everyone thinks Estrada is down here in Lexington when he's still in Washington. . . ?' Madigan let the word trail off. 'Or is he? Is he somewhere else?'

This time Renaldo managed a full grin, although it was fleeting, twisted by a pain spasm. 'He said you were a *hombre intelligente, señor* . . . but are you smart enough?'

'For what?' Madigan demanded, eyes narrowing now. He saw uncertainty wash across the dirty, greasy moon face, but then Renaldo obviously made an effort and said, 'To know where Estrada really is? Or what he is doing?'

'Don't think I have to be, Renaldo,' the marshal said, cocking his Colt again and casually aiming at one of the man's feet. 'Be a helluva life for a man used to lots of activity and getting all the enjoyment he can to have no thumbs, and crippled feet as well . . . take the edge off living, I reckon.'

Kimble stirred but remained silent. The gunfighter turned his head a little to look at Madigan. The marshal saw him, frowned slightly, and then Renaldo claimed his attention again.

'I-I know you can do these things you say, Señor Madigan, and I am afraid.' He could hardly breathe now and his words staggered out singly, some loud, some soft, but he continued doggedly. 'But I must, this is the only way, the only weapon I have . . . You give me your honour to let me go without further harm and I-I will tell what I know. . . . It may not be all you want to know, but I give my word – I tell you everything *I* know. Please? OK?'

'The man's going to have a heart attack in a minute, Bronco! And it's not a bad deal.' Kimble leaned forward avidly.

'Catch your breath Renaldo, then start talking.'

'We-we have a deal?'

'Not yet – after I hear what you say, I'll decide.' Madigan's face was inscrutable now but there was a palpable menace coming from him. 'It's as good a deal as you'll get.'

The Colt's barrel still pointed unwaveringly at the Mexican's nearest boot and suddenly the man's round body quivered all over and he slumped in upon himself and nodded vigorously.

'*Sí, sí*! OK!' He began to talk quickly, words spilling one over the other, as if he was afraid he would not get everything out before something happened to him. Something really bad. And he spoke both Spanish and American.

But before they had sorted out what he was trying to say from the chaos of words mixed with sobs and cries of abject fear, all hell broke loose.

It was Kimble's fault. Concentrating on what Renaldo was trying to tell them, he squatted a couple of feet from the mystery gunfighter. The man seemed limp and listless, only vaguely aware of what was happening around him, his single exposed eye under the crude bandage not focusing properly.

Next thing Kimble knew he was sent sprawling

from a savage blow against the side of his head and through the roaring and spreading red mist, he was vaguely aware that his six-gun had been snatched from his holster.

Madigan, too, was caught unawares, frowning in his own concentration as he tried to make sense of Renaldo's words. But he heard the thump as Kimble fell sprawling and spun instinctively, swinging the Colt away from Renaldo's foot, thumb releasing the hammer spur.

Even so he wasn't fast enough.

Whoever this gunfighter was, he was half-brother to greased lightning and he knew his job – which was that of a cold-blooded killer.

Kimble's Colt in the man's hand seemed to roar in a continuous explosion of sound. The first two shots smashed into Renaldo, spinning the fat little man violently, taking him through the head and the chest. Without pause, the gun barrel twitched in Madigan's direction, spitting flame and smoke and the marshal was slammed over backwards, almost somersaulting, but his body caught halfway through the motion and he crashed on to his side.

The gunman kicked out at Kimble's head as he groggily tried to grab the killer's ankle. But he didn't move the gun from Madigan – he knew where the real danger lay and intended to get rid of it as quickly as possible. Kimble groaned and sprawled awkwardly as the gunfighter stepped forward to fire the killing shot into Madigan.

The marshal was floundering, hit somewhere in the chest, gun arm caught partly beneath his body.

He tried to wrench aside but pain slowed him and even as he dragged the Colt free he knew he wasn't going to make it. The man bared his teeth as he set the six-gun on Madigan and said quite clearly, 'I've waited a long time for this!'

The shot seemed further away than Madigan expected, even as he instinctively tensed his body to accept the impact of the slug. There was a second shot, much closer and something drove into the ground beside him, stinging his face with grit and half blinding him.

By the time Madigan realized he wasn't fatally shot and his vision cleared, the gunfighter was down on his knees, coughing a thin scarlet stream from one corner of his mouth, his shirt front now a spreading red stain. Kimble's gun fell from his opening hand and he swayed before toppling on to one side.

Madigan grunted and struggled to a sitting position, tightening his grip on his own Colt, looking around to see who had shot the mystery man. Kimble was still dazed but coming out of it. Renaldo was beyond anyone's help.

Bronco snapped his head around, ignoring the wave of dizziness, as he heard a sound to his right – and saw Jenny Squires hurrying towards him from the direction of the house, her smoking Henry in her hands.

She was pale and breathless as she ran up, staring down at the gunfighter's bloody figure.

'Oh, God, did I kill him?' she gasped.

CHAPTER 13

THE HUNTER

The first camp was high in the Alleghenies and the two weary marshals ground-hitched their mounts and the spares, then rolled up in their blankets without even a cup of coffee.

Both were awake before first light and Kimble started the fire while Madigan sliced some sowbelly given to them by Jenny Squires. They made breakfast in silence and ate it with only the exchange of a few words. Both men had plenty to think about.

Not the least being why Estrada had sent an impostor south to Lexington.

After the shoot-out, Jenny attended to Madigan's wound – the bullet had passed through the flesh covering the muscle between his arm and his body and while it was hellish sore and had bled plenty, it was far from fatal. As the woman had worked on him, Madigan had berated Kimble for his slackness in allowing the mystery gunfighter to snatch his gun.

146

Before dying, the gunman had talked briefly to Madigan, just enough to allow the marshals to make some startling deductions. Kimble, contrite, was surprised to find that Madigan and the man knew each other.

'Riley Bensinger,' Madigan had announced when he had gotten closer to the barely conscious man. He reached out and tore off the head bandage Kimble had applied: Bensinger would not benefit any from wearing it – or any other bandage. He was already on his last long ride to whatever destiny awaited him and it was downhill all the way.

'You know this Bensinger?' Kimble asked, clearly startled. 'I know the name – he has a reputation for cold-blooded killings – women, children, cripples, anyone!'

'That's him – a fine human being. We've tangled before, haven't we, Riley.' Madigan shook the man, brought groans to the slackening lips and the dulled eyes turned slowly towards him.

'Damn you, Madigan. . . . Finally had my chance . . . at you and . . . I messed-up. . . .' Bensinger coughed and blood sprayed.

'Didn't recognize you at first without the spade beard and moustache,' Madigan said. 'Might've known Estrada would hire some snake like you – but for what?' Bensinger glared and slowly Madigan smiled, although it was the last thing he felt like. He was in plenty of pain from his own wound. 'Let's see, you nailed Renaldo first, although you must've known it was risky, leaving me a chance to get in a shot at you. So, did you kill Renaldo to stop him spilling the beans about Estrada, or did Estrada want him dead at any cost . . . and it was your job to see to it?'

'You're doin' the talkin',' gasped Bensinger.

'That could be it!' Kimble said abruptly, eager to make amends for not watching Bensinger more closely. 'Bronco! Renaldo said it was *imperative* that people thought Estrada was down here in Kentucky when he was really – well, it doesn't matter where for the moment – but suppose the man everyone thought was Estrada was killed. . . ?'

Madigan looked at him sharply, frowning a little, flicking his gaze to Bensinger who was showing signs of agitation as well as surprise. Madigan nodded slowly.

'Was that it, Riley? Poor old Renaldo thought Estrada was giving him an extra bodyguard, taking good care of him, when your real job was to kill him so everyone would think Estrada was dead, huh? That it, you murdering scum?' Madigan smiled coldly. 'Of course it is! Estrada's in a heap of trouble of some kind and daren't go back to Mexico, right? So, he has his stand-in murdered by a known killer-for-hire, and as far as anyone's concerned, that's the end of it – Estrada's dead in Lexington: even his loyal bodyguard, The Hawk, couldn't save him. You'd do your usual disappearing act and no one would bother much about who hired you: just having scum like Estrada dead would be good enough. No one would really care why or who or where. 'Madigan paused. 'Wait up! *Where was* important – but why?'

Bensinger's chest was heaving now and there were

bubbling sounds in his throat. Even the pain twisting his face couldn't hide his discomfort as he listened to Kimble's and Madigan's deductions.

'What's Estrada up to, Riley?' Madigan asked him, but the way he said it, it was obvious he was really thinking out loud. 'Brannigan had the money to pay off someone, maybe several people, in a position to give Estrada protection and a new life. I'll bet there was a heap more to come because hiding a snake like Estrada wouldn't come cheap – Barnes upset things by stealing that cash drawer and the IOUs. The Marshals' investigation into corruption stirred things up even more. Drastic measures had to be taken – and the missing IOU recovered if possible. Jenny had to die in case she'd seen who signed it, so it was a good chance to set-up Estrada's "murder" a long way from Washington where he was being fixed up with a new identity and so on. . . .'

'Bronco.' Kimble spoke softly but there was an intensity in the single word that made Madigan look at him sharply. 'Suppose that man you saw when you were on street patrol and thought was Estrada was only Renaldo in disguise? It could mean the real Estrada never came to Washington at all, maybe never even left Mexico. . . .'

Madigan heaved a sigh. 'Too many "ifs", Beau. Estrada would come in person to arrange something like this when his future depends on it. We need someone in the know to give us the full story.' He was looking at the dying Bensinger and the gunfighter opened his eyes wide. 'Any takers, Riley. . . ?'

Madigan unholstered his Colt and began to check

the loads. Kimble was as stiff as a statue, totally disapproving, not sure whether Madigan was serious or merely just trying to stir up Riley Bensinger and throw a scare into him.

The killer rolled his eyes, having trouble hanging on now. 'Go . . . to . . . hell . . . Mad-i-gan . . .' It took a supreme effort on Bensinger's part and it was his last. After some gurgling and convulsing he slumped back dead.

Bronco sighed, holstered his gun and stood slowly. 'Well, I guess we're stuck with our theories, Beau.' He swayed a little unsteadily. Jenny Squires was at his side, taking his arm, in an instant.

'You'd best come up to the house for some coffee.'

Madigan had no intention of disagreeing with the suggestion. There was a lot of cleaning-up to do here and he needed a stimulant like coffee – or something stronger.

Kimble contacted Sheriff Doucette and put him part-way in the picture and the lawman reluctantly agreed to have a man watch over Jenny Squires. He was a trifle put-out that he wasn't being given the full deal – and itching to do something about Madigan being on his Wanted list. Then, with fresh horses and Jenny's grubsack, they quit town and rode fast and furiously back in the direction of Washington.

There was no choice, really: they didn't know if the real Estrada was there or not. But they both agreed that the signature Jenny had seen on that IOU and deciphered as 'Cottrell' was almost certainly 'Cattrell'.

So, if the senator was involved, even if he had been

blackmailed into it, he was the next man to see.

'I've never heard that Titus Cattrell is a gambler, Bronco,' Kimble said, as they rode through the mountains.

'Me, neither – and even if he is, I can't see him choosing to play with a tin-horn like Deuce Brannigan. Although I've heard Deuce could arrange high-stake games for a price, and he had plenty of takers from the social set.'

Kimble straightened in the saddle, frowning. 'Yes – that's a point.'

Madigan was silent as they rode through a gulch and climbed out on to a more or less flat run towards the next towering range. Just before they reached the mountains' shadow he said, 'But *Randy* has a reputation as a hellraiser, Beau – a game of five-card stud or draw poker, Deuce's specialty, would easily snag a greenhorn like him. Deuce liked to sucker his mark with a high-card opener, then sandbag him with a better hand after he got all excited and pushed the stakes through the roof. If Randy was reckless with Titus's money—'

'By God, Bronco!' Madigan knew immediately Kimble was excited at the idea because of the exclamation. 'It could fit! Emmaline said that her father was mighty angry with Randy for running up gambling debts – he'd settled some minor ones – but swore no more! But if they had Randy's signature on an IOU for a large amount, they could manipulate Titus and force him to do whatever they wanted. A man in his position couldn't afford to have his son in debt to some two-bit gambler – apart from opening the way to embezzlement of public funds, Titus is after that ambassador's job. He'd stand no chance if that IOU was made public.'

Madigan called a halt long enough for them to change saddles to the spare mounts. They prepared to ride all through the night so as to arrive in Washington as early as possible the next day.

The senator had armed guards on his estate and Madigan knew they would stand little chance of getting past them. At least he would: officially, he was still a fugitive.

'Time to earn your keep, Beau.'

Kimble looked at him sharply as they waited in the deep shadows of a clump of elms overlooking the Cattrell place in the early light of pre-dawn. They had covered the distance faster than they had expected. They watched as the guards patrolled the big grounds. Madigan had spotted four but Kimble was sure there were more at the rear. He wasn't happy but sighed and moved forward.

Whatever he said to the guard on the gate seemed to work, for the man undid the padlock and slid the iron rods aside, swinging open the gate. Kimble was as startled as the guard himself when Madigan suddenly crashed past and slammed the side of his gun across the guard's head.

'What're you doing!'

Madigan hurriedly closed the gate, leaving the padlock hanging in its chain but not snapped, the iron rods only just resting on the edge of their sock-ets: could be they might have to leave in a hurry.

Kimble helped move the unconscious guard. They sat him in his small clapboard gatehouse and Madigan slapped his hat over the slack face.

Madigan grabbed Kimble's arm and hustled him into the grove of trees that screened the big house from the curving drive leading in from the street.

'We don't even have a proper plan!' complained Beau.

'Good time to learn how to improvise. Now, shut up, Beau, follow my signals and we'll be in the house in no time.'

'I don't know about this, Bronco! Breaking into a senator's home is bad enough, but someone like Cattrell!'

'Just hope that Parminter backs us up. Now move!'

They were opposite a stone balustraded balcony now with French doors opening on to it, the room beyond hidden by heavy, drawn drapes. Guns in hands, they climbed over the balustrade and crouched by the doors. Madigan had thought he saw a chink of light showing as he crossed the balcony and now, closer, he looked through a narrow gap between the curtains into a lighted room.

It was the senator's study, seemed as big as a hotel foyer to Madigan. Cattrell was seated behind his desk and *El Halcon* stood beside him, his cross-draw gun butts glinting darkly in the lamplight as the senator wrote on some document. He glanced up at the rangy Mexican gunfighter and Madigan could just make out his words.

'This should be ratified by a senate committee and then duplicate documents issued. Anyway, Estrada already has enough papers to see him out of the country. I'm not going to forge something as delicate as this from the State Department—'

The Hawk slammed him hard across the side of the face with his calloused hand, hit his shoulder roughly and pointed to the pen, right hand now resting on one gunbutt. 'You will give me this paper! You sign and fix the seal, *señor*. That will pass any inspection, no?' His voice was cold and merciless. 'Remember, your beautiful daughter is very close if you need further persuasion.'

'You bastard! Leave her out of this!'

The Hawk pointed with a savage motion, back-handed the senator once more. Cattrell swayed and Madigan saw that the pen was shaking badly now. However, he changed his grip, set his shoulders and then signed the paper, set down the pen, and melted some sealing wax in a candle flame and pressed his large signet ring into the warm wax. The Hawk reached past him and snatched up the paper.

'Merely an extra precaution, *señor* – I am loyal to Don Felipe, but perhaps I need special papers, too, eh? *This* paper will open many doors!'

Cattrell twisted in his chair. 'So that's why you had me leave the name space blank . . . now give me my son's IOU.'

The Hawk smiled thinly, placing the folded papers in an inside pocket of his short jacket. 'It would appear that I was not successful in recovering the paper you speak of. Madigan and his young friend reached the woman first.'

Cattrell was on his feet now, face white, fists

clenching. 'My God! *Madigan* knows about it? Damn you, for a lying son of a bitch! I don't care about the other senators your boss has blackmailed into helping him, but you promised me that IOU with Randy's name on it and I want it! I *need* it!' He suddenly lunged for a bell rope. 'Or you won't leave this house alive!'

The Hawk almost languidly pulled one of his guns from leather and Madigan didn't wait. He grabbed the startled Kimble by his shirtfront, and hurled him backwards through the doors. Glass shattered and wood splintered as Kimble tangled in the drapes, dragging them off the rods, slide rings popping one by one. The Hawk stood frozen, but only for a split second. But it was long enough for Madigan to shove Beau roughly aside and dive sideways, his Colt triggering while he was still hurtling into the room.

His shot missed: it was only a diversion anyway. Hawk crouched, his gun hammering as Madigan dropped to the carpet, twisted and rolled across the room, almost into the desk's leg-well. Cattrell had managed to drop out of his chair and crouch low as the Mexican fired over his head at the blurred form of Madigan. The marshal's gun hand swung up beneath the elaborate desk and he fired twice up through the desktop. Two fist-sized hunks of mahogany flew into the air and The Hawk staggered as the flattened bullets drove into his lean body. By then Madigan was up on one knee, firing again. The Hawk spun, wrenched around by the impact, cannoned into the wall and slid down to crumple on the floor.

Kimble helped the shaken Cattrell to his feet. 'It's all right, sir, if you can just tell us where to find Estrada we'll put the final touches to the whole sorry mess.'

Cattrell wrenched free of Kimble's grip and sat himself down. He looked wild-eyed as the other door burst open and three sweating bodyguards stumbled in with guns sweeping around in jerky arcs: Corey, Starke and Tennery. . . .

'Too late!' Cattrell roared. 'I could've been shot ten times over! Get out! You're all fired!' They retreated, slack-jawed. Cattrell turned to Kimble and Madigan. 'Estrada's gone – under the full protection of the United States Government! He can't be stopped now – it would take forever and a day to have his papers rescinded.' He curled a lip bitterly. 'The man's got half of Washington's senators in his pocket thanks to Brannigan's IOUs.'

'We thought there was only one, sir,' Kimble said frowning. 'The one with Randy's name on it.'

'It somehow got left out and Barnes tried to cash in on it. No, Brannigan had six or seven others bearing senators' names, or someone from their families. Forged or not, they could be very very damning and gave Estrada all the power he needs to escape. Randy was a fool to ever—'

'How is the boy, Senator?' Madigan asked flatly, no pretence at politeness or courtesy, but it was a sincere enquiry.

'There's every chance he'll make a full recovery – no thanks to you! And you haven't heard the last of it!'

Kimble, watching closely, saw the relief on Madigan's hard face, although he covered swiftly, seemed untouched by Cattrell's threat.

Cattrell said quietly enough, 'Estrada has sufficient legal papers to give him full diplomatic protection. They were obtained under duress of course, but he *has* them. I didn't realize this last one was for Hawk himself for use when he gets overseas with Estrada.'

Then Kimble stiffened as Emmaline entered the office, a robe over her nightgown. She stopped dead when she saw him, looked at her father, barely gave Madigan a glance, then hurried towards Kimble. Her worried face brightened. 'Oh, Beau! I'm so glad you're safe!'

Madigan turned away as Kimble slid his arm about her waist and they began to speak in low voices. 'Senator, I don't know what's behind all this, but it seems to me Estrada can still be stopped.'

'Not legally. The papers he carries will stand him in excellent stead and get him past any frontier in almost any country friendly to the United States of America. There isn't a court in the land that could delay him now.'

'Hell almighty! What is it he's running from?'

Cattrell said bitterly, 'No need to go into details but suffice it to say Estrada overstepped the mark in Mexico – with *El Presidente* niece.'

Madigan nodded. 'I heard a little about that.'

'The girl took her own life: she was very young, impressionable, the president's favourite, and Estrada thought he could discard her like the dozens

157

of other women he has violated. He ran as far north as he could go, and found his salvation in his friend Deuce Brannigan's list of IOUs, some of which had been used previously to get him concessions that would have been impossible to obtain in any other way.'

'And this time, he had half-a-dozen real live federal senators under his thumb. Powerful ones, like you.'

Cattrell looked down at his bullet-scarred desk, lips pursed. It was as near to showing shame as he ever would and it surprised Madigan a little.

'Just where is Estrada now, Senator?'

Cattrell lifted his eyes slowly. 'There is a ship loading at Quantico docks. It's due to sail down the Chesapeake on the noon tide – bound for South America. It's too late to stop him, Madigan. Too much of a legal tangle. And with those papers, the law can't touch him, anyway.'

'So the son of a bitch is gonna thumb his nose at us all,' Madigan gritted, fire blazing in his eyes. He glared as Kimble and the girl came across, Emmaline smiling as she touched her father's arm. He took her by the shoulders and they spoke together. Madigan looked quizzically at Kimble.

'Wedding on after all?'

Beau looked startled, then smiled, shaking his head. 'No wedding – she wasn't pregnant. False alarm and then in a fit of childish spite she sent that wire to worry me because we'd had a tiff. It's all straightened out now, Bronco. We're ... good friends again.' He frowned. 'You look on edge, like you're eager to get going somewhere.'

'Parminter told me I'm getting old if I let the strain get to me. Maybe he's right. Maybe I'm too old to handle this kind of pressure, Beau.' The admission lifted Kimble's eyebrows. 'Listen, do me a favour: tell Parminter he was right – I couldn't stand the strain any longer so I'm taking a short break – might do a little hunting.'

'What! He won't like that, Bronco. He'll—'

'Can I borrow that Mannlicher of yours?'

'Eh? Oh, I guess so,' Beau said, reluctantly, then smiled in Emmaline's direction. 'I'll stick around town for a bit, I think . . . your wound's bleeding again by the way!'

'Might's well throw in that telescopic sight, too,' Madigan said, with elaborate casualness, ignoring the observation about his wound.

'Well, OK, but it's so powerful it's hardly sporting to use it when hunting.'

'I'm no great sportsman – long as I make the kill.'

Kimble frowned. 'You're up to something, Bronco—'

'Beau! Will you just make your excuses to the girl and get me the damn rifle and 'scope!' He glanced up at the clock on the wall. *It was already 7.50 – at least a two-hour ride to Quantico, then find a suitable place that would give him a clear view of the passenger deck, just on the turn of the tide when it would be steadiest . . .* it was going to be mighty close!

But Madigan figured he could just make it in time if Kimble got a move on.

Beau, peeved, suspecting he was being left out,

said, 'Oh, all right! Come on!'

They strode to the broken French doors, and across the balcony. Madigan didn't bother saying goodbye to the senator. He knew he wasn't finished with Cattrell yet ... and there would be a lot of untangling to do with Parminter, too. But he was confident he could handle it. . . .

'Do you always have to play things so darn close to your chest, Bronco?' Beaumont T. Kimble complained.

'Find I make fewer mistakes that way,' Madigan allowed, taking the finely made Mannlicher rifle that Beau slid from the saddle scabbard. His hands caressed the smooth metal and woodwork, checked the mounts where the telescopic sight would clip on, the slickness of the bolt-action.

He smiled at the frowning Kimble.

'I'll be mighty surprised if I can't hit what I aim at with this, Beau. I prefer one-shot kills.'

'It's not perfect, you know,' Kimble said, a little stiffly. A feeble rejoinder, but he resented Madigan cutting him out of whatever deal he was cooking-up: only later would he realize it was for his own good.

Madigan nodded, not really listening. If, for some reason he missed and the ship sailed away – well, he could always send a wire to *El Presidente.*

He remembered reading once that the great man had large beef interests in Argentina.

No matter what Titus Cattrell and the other black-mailed senators thought, one way or another, Felipe Estrada would be stopped.

Dead.